A TIGHT NOOSE
AND A BLOOD VOW

As the mob prepared to hang him, Ridge Parkman's eyes darted to the spot where Marshal Wyatt Bass had been standing. Now he was nowhere in sight.

Suddenly Ridge smelled a plot. It was possible, he decided, that Bass had actually put these men up to a lynching.

After only a few days in this cattletown, Ridge had stirred up more trouble than he thought possible. But if he lived through this, the grand gunslinging legend of Wyatt Bass would end in a powdersmoke showdown.

RIDGE PARKMAN WESTERN THRILLERS

by Greg Hunt

WHEN LEGENDS DIE

Greg Hunt

A DELL BOOK

Published by
Dell Publishing Co., Inc.
1 Dag Hammarskjold Plaza
New York, New York 10017

Dell ® TM 681510, Dell Publishing Co., Inc.

ISBN: 0-440-19465-2

Printed in the United States of America

First printing—January 1982

WHEN LEGENDS DIE

CHAPTER ONE

The ragged cowboy had long since passed the point of mere drunken rowdiness. He had turned snake mean, unpredictable and totally uncontrollable, and the revolver tied down low on his leg made him a danger to everybody else in the small, crowded saloon.

Marshal Wyatt Emerson Bass was seated at a large round table near the rear of the saloon playing cards with six other men. He sat with his back to the wall so he could look out over the whole room, and he had kept an eye on the cowboy for some time. He was irritated by the distraction of the man's loud, boisterous talk and prodding ways and knew he was going to have to get up and do something soon so they could continue the game in peace.

Bass picked up the cards one by one as they came sliding across the table toward him. Queen. Ten. Nine. Eight. Ten. It was an exasperating hand, and he sat staring for a moment at his cards, debating whether to throw one ten and draw to the risky inside straight or keep the tens and discard the rest.

Out across the room the marshal heard Matt the bartender say firmly but nervously, "You'd best holster that fircarm before somebody gets hurt here, cowboy."

Matt was talking loudly for Bass's benefit, and the marshal knew the time had come.

He laid his hand face down on the table and said calmly to the other players, "Just hold 'em a minute, boys. I got some business to take care of, but it won't take long."

Cards went down around the table and a couple of the players slid their chairs around, so they would have a better view of what was about to happen.

As Bass rose to his full six feet two inches and threw his coattails back to expose the pearl grips of the twin revolvers he wore, the room quieted. Most of the eyes in the saloon turned his way, except those of the drunken cowboy, who kept his pistol waving around wildly, ranting about taking on the whole place.

Despite the muggy heat in the saloon, Bass was dressed in a spotless black wool suit, complete with buttoned vest, white shirt, starched collar, and string tie. He was a striking figure, tall, wide-shouldered, and powerful. His face, with full, carefully trimmed mustache and deep tan, was craggy and handsome.

As he moved slowly and calmly from behind the table, his eyes narrowed to calculating slits and that vague, ominous grin, a trademark of Wyatt Emerson Bass, crossed his face. His hands, hanging casually by his sides, were only inches from his sidearms.

When he stepped toward the center of the room, a tunnel several feet wide opened up between him and the drunken cowboy, who now seemed to be the only person in the saloon who had not noticed Bass. When he spoke, his deep rich voice, though calm and not overly loud, carried the full impact of his authority and considerable reputation. "Put the gun on the bar and step away from it," he said.

The cowboy weaved unsteadily on his feet as he soaked in that something was going on. He looked over his shoulder at Bass, then turned to face him, the revolver pointed squarely at Bass's middle.

"Do it the easy way, cowboy," Bass warned, not the slightest ruffled by the gun leveled at him.

"Go to hell," the cowboy growled. "I've put your kind in the ground from here plumb to Ca–"

The two shots sounded as one and the pistol went flying out of the cowboy's right hand as he spun left and went down. He lay there for a moment, his mouth open in stunned silence, as he surveyed his shattered right hand and left shoulder.

With the acrid black powder smoke still drifting out of their barrels, Bass stylishly twirled the twin revolvers once and holstered them.

"You an' you," he said, pointing to the two men closest to the downed man. "Haul this fool out of here an' down to Doc Elliott's."

As he turned to take his place at the card table, the low rumble of awed discussion was already beginning in the saloon. It would be a story almost every man in the place would tell and retell countless times in the coming years. *The Time Wyatt Bass Shot the Cowboy in the Dixie Darling Saloon.*

The two bystanders grabbed the cowboy by both of his arms, ignoring his howls of pain as they hauled him to his feet, and dragged him from the saloon.

As they passed through the swinging doors, a man slouched down in a chair near the entrance looked at the ugly, bloody hole in the wounded man's shoulder and shook his head. He was stupid, the man thought, but all things considered, he was a lucky cuss, too. Depending on who was doing the telling, Wyatt Emerson

Bass had killed anywhere from twelve to fifty men. He was blurringly fast, unerringly accurate at amazing distances, and absolutely fearless.

The man near the door swirled the last bit of whiskey around in his glass reflectively, gulped it down, caught the eye of one of the saloon girls at the end of the bar, and signaled that he wanted a refill. This was the first time he had ever seen Wyatt Bass in person, but even before arriving here in Cornersville and witnessing the man's prowess, he was reasonably assured that Bass had come by his tremendous reputation the hard, honest way.

A lot of men known as top guns in the West had built their reputations on a lot of backshooting, and often aided their own images with a lot of outlandish bragging. Not so with Bass. He didn't have to boast. Any male over six years old who lived west of the Mississippi River could generally recount the entire legend of this famous lawman.

From the unlikely hometown of Baltimore, Maryland, Wyatt Bass had come West at the age of seventeen to learn the lawman's trade from his older brother Stuart, who was then involved in ramming a little law and order down the unwilling throats of the residents of Salinas, Kansas. After later being joined by a third brother, Morton, the Bass brothers made several moves, working as a team to tame towns nobody else was willing or foolhardy enough to take on.

But the partnership had been broken up in a barrage of gunfire during the legendary bank robbery in Sweet Springs, Kansas, by thorny old Zeb Pennypacker and his gang of Confederate Army outcasts.

Taking only a day and a half to get his two brothers

buried and to pack his gear, Wyatt Bass, then twenty-two years old, had trailed the gang for seven weeks across four states, mercilessly killing them off one by one.

He had finally caught up with Pennypacker himself somewhere in the Dakotas, and when he returned to Sweet Springs, the old rogue's head was dangling in a stinking deerskin bag on Bass's saddle. The head had hung on a spike on a telegraph pole at the edge of town for some time, but finally the local Methodist congregation took a vote one Sunday morning and persuaded Bass to let them take the rotting thing down and bury it at last.

That feat alone had been quite enough to insure Bass a prominent place among the living legends of his day, but in the ensuing thirteen years there had been other great kills to keep the legend growing.

At that poker table across the room was the man who had taken out the three vicious Parson brothers, the man who had hunted down and killed Crazy Joe Moon, the renegade Cherokee who had terrorized half of New Mexico Territory with his insane spree of rape, looting, and slaughter.

There had been other feats and killings, great and small, but now at thirty-five, Bass seemed to have settled in permanently as city marshal here in Cornersville, Kansas. In addition to his comfortable salary of two hundred dollars per month from the town, he also had considerable income from this saloon, which he owned, and from some ambiguous ties with a couple of packing companies which bought the cattle herds coming up out of Texas to be shipped out from the city's railheads.

Sipping from his fresh drink, the stranger kept his gaze on Bass, watched his quick smile appear and fade with the tides of the game, heard the pleasant banter he kept up with his fellow players, and began to get the feel of what sort of man this was.

Bass stayed in the game for more than an hour, but finally around eleven he began to stack up his folding money and to bid the other players good night. On his signal, one of the bar girls came over to gather up his chips. He patted her rump familiarly and gave her a piece of gold, as she started away toward the bar to cash him in. Then he rose, straightened the wrinkles in his vest with a short tug, donned his black hat, and strode toward the door.

The man by the door downed the last of his drink, waited a moment, and then followed Bass out. When he reached the edge of the board sidewalk outside, he looked around and spotted the marshal about fifty feet away, walking up the street in long, ambling strides.

The stranger took a few steps into the street and then called out, "Marshal Bass?"

Bass paused and turned to see who had called to him. His movements were calm and unthreatening, but by the time he completed the turn, his right coat-tail was back and his hand was near his gun. "That's me, all right," he answered. "What can I do for you, friend?"

As he started toward Bass, the man said, "I'd be obliged if you could spare me a minute or two." When he reached Bass, he said, "The name's Ridge Parkman. Deputy U.S. Marshal."

"Glad to meet you," Bass said, taking Parkman's hand with a firm grip and shaking it. "Come on with me up to the office, an' we can take all the time you need."

Bass led the way down the street and into a one-story brick building with barred front windows. The front room of the office contained two desks, a long bench, and a pot-bellied stove near one wall. In a locked case on one side were several rifles and shot-guns, and a barred door in the middle of the back wall led to the cell area.

Sitting, and leaning back in a chair with his feet up on a desk, was a handsome young man of about twenty. He wore a holstered pistol, held a rifle in his lap, and had a bright gold star pinned above the breast pocket of his clean white shirt.

"That's brother Bill there," Bass told Parkman as they entered the office. "Get up, Billy, an' shake the hand of Deputy U.S. Marshal Ridge Parkman."

Billy laid the rifle aside and shook Ridge's hand warmly, saying, "Welcome, Mr. Parkman."

Bass pulled a chair up for Parkman and then went around and sat down behind the larger of the two desks. "Billy, go wake Mabel up an' tell her to make us some coffee an' bring it down here," he said. "Then you better make a door check, an' stop by Doc Elliott's to see when we can bring that feller down here an' throw him in the lockup."

"What feller's that, Wyatt?" Billy asked, picking up his rifle to leave.

"I had a little trouble down at the Dixie," Bass said. "Some drifter's got a couple of brand new holes in him, but nothin' too serious. I was wonderin' why you didn't come down there to check out the shots. Must of caught you napping."

"I wasn't napping," Billy said seriously. "I went

down to the stables awhile ago to check on that bad hoof my horse's got. Maybe the noise from the cattle pens kept me from hearin' the shots."

"Sure, Billy. I was just razzin' you. It wasn't nothin' I couldn't handle all right."

"Okay, I'll go take care of those things for you," Billy said. "Nice meeting you, Marshal."

When he had gone, Bass explained, "My baby brother. Just come out from back East a few months ago, but he's goin' to make a damn good lawman."

"How could he miss with the teacher he's got?" Parkman said.

Bass accepted the compliment without comment. "So what brings a U.S. marshal to our little town?" he asked.

"I've come after a man that killed an Army colonel down to El Paso," Parkman said. "Seems he got crazy one night and put a bullet in the side of the colonel's head, but they didn't get him on the spot. El Paso wired up to Kansas City that he was headed up this way an' I jus' happened to be around at the time the wire came in. They sent me down to pick him up an' get him back to El Paso."

"Be glad to help you out," Bass offered. "Just tell me who it is an' I'll have Billy go pick him up for you."

"I can take my man, all right," Parkman said. "This is just a courtesy call so you'll know which side I'm on in case the lead starts flyin'. I don't like the idea of bein' laid out by the local lawman 'fore I could explain myself, 'specially when the local law is Wyatt Bass."

"It's a good idea you stoppin' by, I guess, especially

since you don't wear a badge. By the way, speakin' of badges, would you mind . . . ?"

"Sure." Ridge grinned, pulling his badge out of an inside pocket and dropping it on the desk in front of Bass. "I jus' don't pin the damn thing on too often. It gets in the way sometimes, an' it seems to make a tempting target. S'pose I don't need to be tellin' you 'bout that part of it, though."

"Nope."

"I also got this warrant," Parkman said, pulling out a folded paper and handing it across to the city marshal. "It's all legal an' proper. Signed by a federal judge in Kansas City."

Bass took the warrant and unfolded it. As he read it, a scowl slowly melted across his face. Finally he looked up at Parkman and asked, "You came here to arrest Ned Rakestraw?"

"That's the man," Parkman confirmed. "The word was he's the trail boss for a Texas outfit pushin' a herd up to the railhead here."

"Ned Rakestraw's been bringin' herds up for the Circle Bar G for eight or ten years. It's one of the biggest outfits in southwestern Texas, an' he's one of the most popular foremen on the trail."

"Popular men get in trouble, too, when they go to makin' corpses out of Army officers," Parkman said.

"He's also a friend of mine," Bass added. "A close personal friend." His tone was guarded and hard to interpret. Parkman stared at his fellow lawman for a moment, the first signs of firm determination and authority beginning to enter his gaze.

Their silent impasse was interrupted as a woman pushed the door open and came in carrying a coffeepot and a plate covered over with a small white cloth. "Wyatt Bass, it seems like you could fire up your own coffeepot," she complained, "instead of having that kid brother of yours drag me out of bed in the wee hours to make coffee for you." She was a short, middle-aged woman with a hefty build and a firm body. Her face was rather plain and unimpressive, but it also contained a certain glow of character and determination which Ridge found attractive. Though she was scowling at Bass now in mock anger, it was easy to see in her eyes the fondness she had for him.

"Good old Mabel," Bass said, his jovial attitude returning suddenly and completely.

"You can forget that 'good old Mabel' stuff, Buster," Mabel complained as she set the pot on the desk and poured two steaming cups of coffee for the men. "Hauling me out of bed at this hour . . ."

"That wouldn't by any chance be a couple of your famous fried pies on that plate, would it?" Bass asked.

"They're leftovers," Mabel said. "Stale and maybe moldy. I only brought them down here hoping you might choke on one and get out of my hair for good and forever."

"You can't fool me, Mabel. I know besides bein' your best customer, I'm also your favorite boyfriend."

"Sure, Wyatt. I need a bundle of trouble like you for a boyfriend just like I need another left foot. All you are is two guns and a stomach with no bottom to it."

Bass leaned across the desk and took a hold of her arm, saying, "Now come around here an' give me some sugar 'fore you leave."

"I'll give you a kiss with my fourteen-inch frying pan. I'd rather snuggle the south end of a northbound mule." She pulled her arm free and marched to the door.

When she was gone, Bass pushed the plate of pastry across to Ridge and said, "You've got to try one of these, Parkman. Best fried pies I've eaten since I pulled my feet out from under Mama's table."

Parkman picked up one of the pies and took a bite. It was a welcome treat after the sparse rations of the trail.

Bass took the second pie and went to work on it with zest. "Now, deputy," he said, washing a big mouthful of pie down with a slug of coffee. "Let's go over this thing one more time an' maybe we can get it straightened out."

"Seems to me it's all clear an' simple enough, Marshal Bass," Parkman said. "I've got to take this Rakestraw feller in. Friend or no friend, he killed himself an Army man an' he's gotta pay the fiddler."

"I wish it was that simple, Parkman," Bass said. The flash of anger he had shown when he first read the warrant had passed now, but Parkman did not like this calm, condescending tone any better. "Let's forget for a moment that Rake's my friend or that I ever even laid eyes on him. There's still some mighty big problems with this thing."

"I'm listenin'."

"There's upwards of 200,000 Texas beeves pass through the loading chutes of Cornersville every year," Bass explained. "We're the last Kansas town where the Texas cattle haven't been banned because of the tick fever they carry, an' that trade is the lifeblood of this town. Without it, this place would be a ghost town within three months. So when the herds come an' the trail hands are in town, folks hereabouts are mighty good to 'em. The town gets rowdy an' there's considerable hell raised while they blow the trail dust out, but we just sorta let it happen an' try to keep a loose lid on the whole thing."

"What's that got to do with takin' Rakestraw in?" Parkman asked, tiring of Bass's long explanations.

"Well, these Texas drovers, they're a clannish lot. They stick like family, an' when you take one of 'em on, you've more than likely taken on the whole bunch. If they got riled, they could jerk this town up by its roots an' scatter it out over half of Kansas."

"I can't see that happenin' to Wyatt Bass's town," Parkman said skeptically.

His own ego and the point he was trying to make clashed in Bass's mind, and he did not answer Parkman immediately. Then he tried a different tack. "How many men have you ever killed, Parkman?" he asked.

Parkman frowned. "It ain't a thing I take a pride in keepin' count of."

"I know. I know," Bass nodded with understanding. "I feel the same way about it. But I've had to do some killing in my day, an' I do take a pride in the fact that I never put a bullet in no man that didn't need killin'. Ned Rakestraw is the same cut of man as that. What about that colonel? Maybe he drawed down on Ned an' forced him to shoot. Who knows what happened? It's not just black an' white."

"He'll get a trial an' that's the place where those things will be decided. It sounds almost like you're tryin' to convince me to pack my gear an' head back without doin' what I came to do."

"It might be the smartest thing."

"You're a lawman an' you know I can't do that," Parkman said. "Would you?"

Bass did not answer the question. His only movement was a slight grinding of his teeth as he stared at Parkman for a long, silent moment.

Finally he said, "Deputy, I've got two obligations in the job I hold here. One is to the law, an' one is to the town. Both are powerful strong. Your mind's set—I can see that plain enough—so it ain't no use us jawin' over this thing any longer. But let me tell you one thing as one lawman to another. When you go after Ned Rakestraw, you've never seen no trouble like you're goin' to stir up. When you rob the hive, you've got to face the bees."

CHAPTER TWO

Parkman took a small room in the back of a cantina in the Mexican part of town. It wasn't much, just a cot in an eight-by-ten room, with one window that didn't open and a door that wouldn't quite close. But the price was right, and it was really all the lawman needed anyway. That dollar twenty-five a day living allowance the government paid didn't stretch far enough to include many luxuries, and he was damned if he would use any of his own money out in the field like this.

It was some time past midnight when he finally got settled into the room. The short, sweaty proprietor who had showed Ridge to the room and lit the candle let him know that he did not necessarily have to sleep in this room alone if he did not want to. It went without saying that there would be at least one willing woman around somewhere in a place like this, but she wouldn't exactly be the type a guy would be anxious to carry home to meet the folks. The offer didn't interest Ridge.

Sleep was what interested him, and when the proprietor left, Ridge quickly shucked his clothes, blew out the stubby candle, and piled down on the cot with his Colt Peacemaker to keep him company. Even the heat and the musky odor of other sleepers that clung to the straw tick did not keep him from enjoying the relaxing feeling of finally being out of the saddle and off of his feet.

Parkman was disgruntled with the whole deal. He wasn't even supposed to be here. He was supposed to be in Denver enjoying the four-day leave that was due him after the last job he had completed. He had earned that four days fair and square, spending as much as sixteen hours a day in the saddle for the past two weeks. His quarry had been Pop Seephus and his two half-wit sons, and Ridge had tracked them across half a dozen backwater Kansas towns before finally arresting them outside Leavenworth and carrying them on down to Kansas City to turn them in.

But things never quite seemed to work out like they were supposed to. That went with the occupation.

Only the purest rotten luck had put him in the U.S. Marshal's office in Kansas City just as the wire came in about Ned Rakestraw and the arrest that had to be made in Cornersville. If it had come half an hour later, he would have already been out in town searching for a steak dinner before starting back to Denver, and Captain Thomlinson of the Kansas City office would have had hell to pay finding him to give him this "little errand."

"Just swing through there and pick him up," Thomlinson had told him casually, as if the trip south to Cornersville was nothing more than a minor detour from the route back to Denver. "An' while you're that far south anyway, you might as well just drop him off in El Paso for trial."

No sweat, Ridge thought. Just take two weeks or a month and ride several hundred miles out of your way across some of the driest, hottest territory in the West. Don't worry about your days off. You'll get them . . . one of these days.

It was a crazy business, and sometimes he thought he was crazy for staying in it, but it was his life and he knew no other. Thomlinson had needed a man and he had been there. That had brought him here, dead tired from five days of hot dirty riding, so exhausted he could not even go to sleep, and half ready to go into the next room and stuff about three-quarters of his left boot down the throat of whoever was snoring so loudly over there.

The one bright spot in the assignment had been the anticipation of meeting, and perhaps working with Wyatt Emerson Bass. Generally Parkman did not put much stock in reputations. Too often the men behind the big names were not nearly as tough or fast or honest or deadly as their legends depicted them to be. And a lot of the best lawmen Parkman knew had names that were not even household words in the next county down the line.

But Bass was a whole different creature altogether. He had come by his reputation fair and square, building it with deeds and not a lot of hot air and exaggeration; he had a right to wear it proudly. It had been a downright pleasure to sit in that saloon tonight, studying Bass and watching the agility and calm competence with which he went about his job. But even that pleasure had been tarnished by what happened later. Parkman had yet to chew over and figure out what exactly had transpired between him and Bass when the name of Parkman's quarry came up, but he was getting one hell of a bad feeling about this whole situation. It was like sitting down to a big pretty steak cooked just right, and then turning it over and finding the underside soft and rotten.

But that was the way it was, and Ridge knew he would just have to live with it. He would get his man, with or without Bass, or even if Bass tried to stop him. It was what he did for a living, and even if he didn't have a name known widely across the West, he was damn good at what he did.

Sleep finally came in stages as he began to force all the pressures and hassles of his work out of his mind and tried to concentrate on more peaceful subjects, like what a man might be able to do with four free days and a couple of months pay in a busy little city like Denver. After all these weeks of solid work and constant, daily danger, his nerves were getting strung out like a taut clothesline, and he recognized that as a dangerous situation for a man in his profession. Nervous men made mistakes, and lawmen who made mistakes had an unsettling habit of dying suddenly. He needed that time off.

Mabel Cain's Café was located midway down Main Street only a few doors away from the city marshal's office. The following morning Ridge found it without difficulty, and after a week of sparse trail rations, he relished the thought of sitting down to a hearty breakfast prepared by a cook with the obvious talents of this lady.

The night in the back room of the cantina had been something less than totally restful. On three separate occasions his sleep had been interrupted by shots somewhere outside, and in the early hours of the morning a drunken cowboy had entered his room, determined that the bed belonged to him for the night. Finally, the logic of Ridge's right fist was the only reasoning the staggering Texan would pay any attention to.

· But in between interruptions, he had been able to knock the edge off his tiredness with a few hours of rest, and when he rose the next morning, he was again ready to take on whatever came along.

Mabel's Café was in a deep, narrow building wedged in between a hardware store on one side and the Drover's Stop Saloon on the other. It was still early in the morning and only one of the twenty or so tables in the place was occupied. The jostling noisy crowds common to cattle towns would not accumulate until later, perhaps around noon, when the cowboys who had spent the previous night carousing and drinking finally began rolling out of their blankets and coming back to life. Right now Cornersville was not much different than any other sleepy little western settlement, but Ridge knew that by midafternoon the town would again be well on its way to living up to its reputation as the most explosive cow town in Kansas.

As Ridge entered, the two men at the table midway back in the room looked up and surveyed him briefly before returning to their conversation. One was a middle-aged, prosperous-looking man, dressed in a striped suit with a neatly brushed derby hat resting on a vacant chair beside him. The other wore worn denims and a flannel shirt, with a broad neckerchief tied around his neck and a revolver and holster tied down on his right leg. From their talk, Ridge quickly picked up on the fact that one of them was a cattle buyer and the other had just pushed a herd up the trail from Texas. In the heat of their negotiations, they did not even seem to notice as Ridge pulled out a chair and took a seat a few tables away.

In a moment Mabel came through the back doorway carrying four plates of food that sent a delicious aroma across the room to the hungry lawman. In each hand she held a platter with a steak so big it hung off both ends, and on each of her forearms was balanced a second plate with three eggs, biscuits, hash browns, and grits.

Mabel threw a smile in his direction, and after she had set the food in front of the drover and cattle buyer, she came over to his table to greet him.

"You're up and about early today, Marshal," she said. "Wyatt must not have bent your ear too late last night."

"It's habit with me," Ridge told her with a grin. "I get to feelin' kinda no 'count if I lay up in the blankets too long after the sun comes up."

"I'm an early riser myself," Mabel said, and then she added with a spark of genial resentment in her voice, "though it don't help the disposition of a woman my age none to be hauled out of bed in the middle of the night to whip up a danged snack for a sassy lawman."

"It looks to me," Ridge told her, "like Marshal Bass pretty much gets what he wants when he wants it around this town. It must be a pretty good arrangement for him."

"Well, can you imagine a body telling him no?" Mabel asked. "It might be something he'd remember the next time some drunken bum of a Texas beef-buster decided to come in and break the place up. And besides," she added with a mock frown, "with that appetite of his, I'd lose about a third of my income if he decided to quit eating in my place."

"Well, ma'am, if those fried pies are any sign of the

way you sling chow, you can count on me bein' a steady customer too as long as I'm in town."

"I can whip up some middling eats when I'm of a mind," Mabel confirmed modestly. "Hell, I've been doing it all my life, one place or another. I had to. I was always too ornery to get married and too dog-faced to work the saloons, so I had to do something to get by. I've had this place four years now, and ain't nobody died on me yet . . . 'least not any that I've heard about. What'll it be for you this morning?"

"I guess you could fill up a gallon bucket with coffee an' bring that out for starters," Ridge told her. "An' then cook me up some steak an' eggs like you brought those men over there. It looked so good I had half a mind to go over an' whip one of them so I could take his."

"You got it, Marshal," Mabel told him.

When she left his table, Ridge took a moment to survey the other men in the room more closely. They were still deep in conversation as they started in on the huge plates of food in front of them, so they paid him no attention. From what he could gather, the buyer was trying to keep his per-head buying price low by pointing out to the drover how many cattle were expected to arrive in Cornersville this season. But the drover was an obvious old hand at this dickering business, too.

"Why, Amos Raintree would run me outa Texas on a rail if I went back an' told him I'd sold his herd off for the price you're offerin'," the cattleman told his companion. "Hell, we coulda sold them to the Indian Agency for damn near that much, an' not had to go to the trouble of shovin' 'em all the way up here to Kansas. You're jus' plain out full of beans, Burke."

"Well, it's his own dadblamed fault for not con-
tracting early with me last fall like I told him to,"
the buyer countered. Neither man was really angry
despite the outward appearances of hostility and stub-
bornness. It was all part of the ritual of bartering, and
both knew they would eventually reach a price that
was mutually satisfactory.

"You know, Amos Raintree hasn't got the only lot
of longhorns for sale in Kansas," Burke continued.
"Word's out the Circle Bar G herd is no more than a
couple of hundred miles down the trail, and they say
Ned Rakestraw's pushing the best lot of steers ever to
leave the Lone Star State."

At the mention of the Circle Bar G, Ridge began
paying much closer attention. Up until now, he had
only a vague idea when Rakestraw might reach Cornersville, and he recognized this as valuable information.

"Yeah," the drover said, "an' we both know Rake
always markets his beef to the outfit Wyatt Bass tells
him to, so don't go tryin' to pull that worn out ol'
crap on me, Burke. This is you an' me doin' business
now, an' it don't make no nevermind if them beeves
Rake brings in here two weeks from now are fat as
buffalo. You up your price, or you can stuff your
money an' hit the pens lookin' for some other sucker
to hoodwink."

The little piece of information Parkman had overheard was disappointing. He had not anticipated having to wait that long for Rakestraw to reach Cornersville, and the prospect of spending as much as two
weeks here was about as appealing as bedding down
in a bear's den and waiting for its owner to come home.
Of course he knew he could always ride out on the

trail and meet Rakestraw on the way up, but there were two main flaws in that idea. For one thing, he disliked the idea of snatching a trail boss away from his herd before it had reached its destination. Doing something like that could spell disaster for the owners back in Texas, and Parkman had no desire to bring about anybody's ruin if he could help it.

And he was also practical enough to realize what a tough job it would be to take Rakestraw and hold him prisoner way out on the trail like that. Chances were that Rakestraw would have a dozen or more men with him who would back him to the bitter end, and Parkman had no delusions about being able to take on that big an outfit all alone. He had not stayed alive this long by doing such stupid things as that, and he did not particularly relish the idea of having his body dumped in a ravine somewhere on the north Texas prairies with thirty or forty bullets in it. The wait would be a nuisance, but if he did wait, he stood a much better chance of getting his man and staying alive in the bargain.

Soon Mabel came out and set his meal in front of him, and then she settled in a chair across the table from him to talk while he began eating.

"You know," she said, "we don't see much of any outside lawmen here in Cornersville. Even the county sheriff over to Nichewood doesn't find his way into town very often since Wyatt took over."

"I can see why," Ridge told her. "With Wyatt Bass in charge, a town generally doesn't need much more in the way of policin'. Jus' his name alone is goin' to keep a lid on a lot of trouble, an' from what I've seen he's well able to handle 'bout anything that comes along without any help."

"He's done a good job here," Mabel confirmed. "Before he came, this town had gone all to hell. When the herds came in, the cowboys just took over. Wasn't nobody safe for six months out of every year, and it was just a disgrace some of the things that happened . . . people getting killed every time you turned around, and the wild ones pretty much getting away with anything they pleased. He changed all that . . . but still . . ."

When she paused, Ridge looked up from his plate, sensing that she had more to say but was not quite sure whether she could trust him or not. "It still ain't always a honeymoon with him here, huh?" he prompted.

"Something like that," she said hesitantly.

"It's that way with these town tamers sometimes," Ridge said. "When they come in an' clean up a place, then they feel like the town is their own personal property, an' they can do anything they want with it. I seen it before."

"We all figured he'd just stop the stealing and the killing and suchlike," Mabel said, lowering her voice nervously so she would not be overheard by the men at the table nearby. "He done that, and everybody's grateful to him for it. But it's hard to overlook some of the other, like the deals he makes with the cattlemen, and the way he treats people like the farmers in these parts when they try to stand up for themselves against the drovers."

"I heard he's got his fingers in the beef business, too," Ridge said, "but I didn't know if it was true or not."

"I'm not quite sure how he works it," Mabel said,

"but somehow or another, he gets a cut when a herd happens to get sold to a couple of particular Kansas City packers. It's not like what he was doing hurt anybody here directly, but still . . . well, me and some of the other folks in town have our doubts sometimes."

"I don't s'pose it's exactly illegal," Ridge told her, "but I know it's bound to make you wonder."

"It does," Mabel said. "But we all know we need him, so we just put up with the things we don't like and generally keep our traps shut. Without Wyatt here, inside of three months Cornersville would switch back to the same hellhole it was before he came. We all know that."

One of the men at the other table signaled for Mabel, and she rose and went over. The cattle buyer gave her some money, which she carried into the back, and then the two men rose rose and left the café. In a minute Mabel came back out and rejoined Ridge.

Parkman found himself liking this independent little woman. True to her own description, she was a mite bit dog-faced, and her build was not exactly the type that would set a man's heart to working overtime. She looked to be past forty, and her prime years were definitely behind her. But she had a certain fire and outspoken determination that he found attractive. She looked like she could hold her own against anything that got slung in her direction, and she was obviously the kind of woman who could make her own way in the world and do a pretty good job of it, too.

Ridge felt relaxed in her company and was glad when she returned to continue their conversation.

"So tell me a little about yourself, Marshal," she said. "Where do you call home?"

"Denver, I reckon," Ridge said. "But most times, I stay on the move. Sometimes I don't flop down on my own bed for a couple of months or more."

"It's strange, living like that, isn't it? I know I used to move around a bit myself, but I always wanted to put a stop to it and make my stand in one place, like I finally got around to doing here."

"A man gets used to it so's he don't hardly know no other way after a while," he said.

"No family?"

"None to speak of."

"It's curious," Mabel admitted. "Don't you ever get the urge to put some roots down somewheres and just hang them guns on a hook behind the door? Don't you ever think about when you get old, where you'll be and what you'll be doing?"

"I'll jus' be proud to live long 'nough to get old, I reckon," Ridge told her with a grin. "The way I look at it, if I do all right an' stay alive clean through every day as it comes, then them times'll take care of themselves when they happen. I can't see much use in spendin' all my younger days figurin' out how to spend my older ones."

"You're an odd one without a doubt, Ridge Parkman," Mabel told him bluntly. "I seen that the first time I laid eyes on you last night, and I think maybe that's how I come to like you so quick. We're pretty much the same, almost like we was cut out of the same bolt of yard goods."

They were again interrupted when four bleary-eyed cowboys strode in the front door and dropped heavily into seats around a big round table near the front. As Mabel was up taking their orders for breakfast, three more men came in and sat down. Ridge had already finished his own meal, and he saw that things were about to get busy for Mabel. He slugged back the rest of the coffee in his mug, caught Mabel to pay the bill, and left the café.

Outside the streets of Cornersville were beginning to fill up, too, but it seemed to be the time of day when the more settled elements of town came out to do their business before the cowboys and drovers woke up and began claiming possession of the town again. For a few chaotic months every year, the permanent residents of Cornersville had learned to structure their living habits around the men who brought the life-giving rush of big herds and big money to their little town.

No matter what else might be said about Cornersville, Kansas, ever since the first trader threw up a sod hut and began selling gunpowder, lead, canned beans, and rotgut whiskey twenty years before, it had never been a dull place to live. In its infancy the town had been a trading center and shipping point for the hundreds of thousands of skins and tons of meat harvested by the buffalo hunters who worked the area mercilessly until it had been decimated of the incredibly large buffalo herds that had once roamed these prairies.

But when the area had been stripped of its most plentiful animal resources, another sort of herd began arriving to keep the town thriving. Events in Kansas had been working for the benefit of Cornersville for more than a decade, and by the late 1870s all the circumstances were right to make the town one of the most thriving, wide-open cattle shipping centers the West would ever know.

During the early years of the decade, more and more towns and cities in the northern and central part of the state fell in behind the shifting quarantine line, which was designed to keep the tick fever carried by the Texas longhorns from infecting the domestic cattle of the state's permanent residents. At last, only Cornersville and a small surrounding area in the southwest part of the state was left open to the vast herds which were brought northward from May to November every year in search of a railhead.

The merchants and businessmen fought long and hard in the state legislature to keep their town open for longhorns because the cattle trade was making all of them rich. Cattle meant a thriving railhead, packed holding pens, and scores of rowdy cowboys with two and three months' pay burning holes in their pockets.

But having the cattle trade also meant making certain concessions to the men who brought the cattle north. A town had to be filled with all sorts of pleasures before the cowboys could work up much interest in coming there. In that respect Cornersville met the test. The boldest of the town's leaders almost touted their disreputable image, sending scouts out on the major trails to assure drovers that the town would be theirs when they arrived, and blatantly encouraging all manner of entertaining vices to flourish.

Into this environment stepped Wyatt Emerson Bass, the ideal lawman for such a place. Within a few months his own personal finances and his duties as town marshal had become so intermingled that often it was nearly impossible to tell whether he was working harder to bring law and order to the town or to keep it as wild and woolly as it had always been.

His saloon, the Dixie Darling, was a perfect example of this double standard. On the one hand, it was one of the rowdiest gambling casinos, saloons, and brothels in the state, but at the same time Bass did his utmost to make sure that at least a loose lid was kept on the exuberant violence of the Texas cowboys when they visited there. When the inevitable fights began, he tried to make sure that as few people as possible were injured or killed and that the guilty parties drew just the right amount of jail time to calm them down a bit. Occasionally a few of the most blatant lawbreakers were sent away to prison or ceremoniously hung, but often Bass preferred merely to shuttle them quickly out of town and bar them from coming back, at least until the next season. It was the kind of law enforcement the Texans could understand, and the kind the residents of Cornersville could tolerate.

But though cattle and the men who herded them still ruled the streets of Cornersville, the protests from the farmers who cultivated the soil in the outlying areas around the town were becoming angrier and more insistent. Everything about the cattle business seemed to infuriate them. When the herds started arriving, fences were routinely cut, watering holes were drained by the thirsty longhorns, pastureland was decimated, and local cattle began dying of tick fever again. When the Texans were in town, the streets of Cornersville were no longer safe places for the farmers' wives and children, and if any local farmer had the audacity to stand up for himself to one of the rowdy Texans, he often found grim retribution coming his way from a whole trail outfit.

Bass's sympathy and apparent alliance with the cattle business was only more salt on the wounds of the indignant farmers. They, as much as anybody else, had looked forward to his coming as a sort of salvation from the wildness that had possessed their town for so long, but they now viewed him as more a part of the problem.

The money and power in southwest Kansas were still centered in the towns and so the herds kept coming, but the farmers bided their time, watched their numbers grow, and carefully hoarded their resources, knowing that someday the endless steel arteries of the railroads would push on south, across the Indian lands and right into the heart of Texas itself. When that happened, the cattle trade to Cornersville would wither and theirs would be the trade that the leaders of Cornersville would have to seek in order to survive.

CHAPTER THREE

Ridge began strolling around town, learning the streets and alleys and buildings. He had never visited Cornersville before, and now since he had the time, he decided he might as well learn what he could about how the place was laid out. If it came down to a fight, a familiarity with the town would be a great advantage, and since Rakestraw had been here many times before, he would already know the place fairly well.

Cornersville was split into two sections by the vital railroad tracks which ran roughly in an east to west direction through the heart of town. North of the tracks, in what was generally considered to be the more respectable side of town, were the larger businesses, professional offices, and the homes of the more settled and affluent members of the community. The south side was where most of the fun was to be found, in the saloons, casinos, and brothels. There were only a few exceptions such as Bass's Dixie Darling Saloon, which was just to the north of the tracks near the dozens of acres of cattle-holding pens.

After a cursory examination of the north part of town, Parkman crossed the tracks and began a more thorough tour of the red light district. It would be here that Rakestraw and his crew would congregate soon after their arrival in Cornersville, and if a confrontation occurred, it would undoubtedly be in this part of town.

The area was familiar, and not unlike the red light districts Parkman had seen in countless other cattle and mining towns all over Kansas, Colorado, Texas, and Nebraska.

Ridge walked the section from one end to the other twice. He was about to turn and head back to the livery barn where he had left his horse stabled, when a voice called out to him loudly from behind.

"Marshal Parkman! Wait up."

Ridge turned and saw Billy Bass nearly a block away from him and walking quickly in his direction. As he waited, he was surprised to see the friendly expression on the younger man's features as he approached. After all, the lines seemed to be forming very quickly here in town. Wyatt Bass had made his stand on Ridge's mission here quite clear the night before, and there was no reason for Ridge to believe that the city marshal's younger brother and deputy would not be in complete agreement with him.

And yet Ridge's initial impression of Billy Bass had been a favorable one, and if the young man wanted to be friendly, Ridge would do nothing to discourage him. He could use all the friends he could get in this place.

"Mornin'," Billy said, greeting Ridge with a grin and a friendly handshake. He was a rather handsome youth in his early twenties with a tall, broad-shouldered build only slightly less statuesque than that of his older brother. "I didn't expect to see you out so early in the morning."

"I'm generally a pretty early riser," Ridge said.

"But I'm just as surprised to see you out an' about at this hour. Seems like you were at work pretty late last night."

"Yeh, the job's got some rugged hours," Billy said. "An' Wyatt, well, he doesn't cut me much slack just 'cause I'm his kid brother an' all. Prob'ly if anything, he makes it rougher on me to compensate for that. But I manage. Hell, I was weaned on the letters from my brothers about their adventures out West, an' since I was just a kid, I wouldn't have considered doing anything else but coming out here an' pinning on a badge when I got old enough. I love it."

"It can get in a man's blood," Ridge agreed. "But it can spill some of it for him, too, if he ain't careful."

"I was just finishing my check on the south side," Billy told him. "You're welcome to walk along if you're not headed anyplace in particular. Usually it's all pretty quiet down here at this time of day, but in a town like Cornersville, you never can tell for sure."

"Sounds fine to me," Ridge said. "I was jus' out doin' a little explorin' myself."

They walked on down another block, then took a left that led them into the heart of the main saloon district. The street was littered with empty bottles, cans, and other debris, but was empty of people except for half a dozen horsemen who had just dismounted a couple of blocks away and were tying their horses to the rail in front of one of the saloons.

As they strolled along the wide board sidewalk at a casual pace, Billy said, "My brother tells me you came here to take Ned Rakestraw back to El Paso to stand trial."

"That's right," Ridge said. For a moment he said nothing more, wanting Billy to reveal a little more about how he felt about the situation. There was no need of getting into a repeat of last night's tense confrontation if it could be avoided.

"It's a mighty tall order you've got for yourself," Billy said. "I think I'd rather be stuck in a cage with a hungry cougar than to take on a whole trail outfit singlehanded an' expect to come out of it alive. But I guess you already know what you're facin'."

"I got a pretty good idea, an' I'll confess it ain't somethin' I'm exactly lookin' forward to."

Billy paused for a moment, then said, "Wyatt says you can't do it. He says when you go out there alone to get Rakestraw, Ned an' his men'll gun you down in the street like a dog."

"There's a fair chance he's right about that, but there ain't much that's certain for a man in life," Ridge said. "We'll see what happens when it happens, I reckon."

Billy seemed to absorb every word Ridge said gravely, and then to carefully consider his own answers. Ridge could not quite figure out how the young deputy felt about this situation, but he was beginning to think that Billy was experiencing some divided loyalties.

"I've got some problems when I start to mull this thing over," Billy admitted finally. "You know, Wyatt's always lectured me that the law is all-important in our work, an' that a good lawman has to be willing to lay down his life for what he thinks is the right thing to do. But he also says that a lawman has to use some good sense in his work, too, an' that knowing when to back off an' take a good hard look at a situation is important sometimes if a man wants to stay alive. I think he's right about you bein' out-gunned by Rakestraw an' his bunch."

"A man'd have to be just a plain-out, addle-headed fool to get himself into the kind of mess I've got into, wouldn't he?" Ridge asked.

"Seems like," Billy said, his brow knit in consternation. "An' yet . . ."

Parkman was glad to hear that "an' yet" tacked onto the end of Billy's statement. It meant he understood why Ridge felt the need to go on with the job despite the tough odds.

A commotion in front of them interrupted their conversation, and for an instant they stopped to see what the six horsemen ahead of them were up to. After tying their horses, the cowboys had gone up to the doors of a nearby saloon, but had apparently found them locked. One of them had begun pounding on the doors and loudly demanding that they be admitted for a drink. He seemed to be arguing with somebody inside.

As they watched, the cowboy at the door pulled his pistol and said, "Either you open up, or I'll bash this damn glass in an' open the place up my own self. I'm thirsty, dammit!"

Billy studied the situation a moment, then said to Ridge, "Hold on a minute an' let me check this out."

As Billy went up to the six men, Ridge walked up to within about fifteen feet and then stopped, realizing that Billy needed to handle this by himself if possible. But as he stood there, Ridge reached down casually and loosened the leather thong which held his Peace-maker in place.

"The man's got a right to open an' close when he

wants to," Billy reasoned casually with the man at the door. "No law here says he has to sell you a drink if he don't want to."

The cowboy scarcely gave Billy a sideways glance as he waved his pistol angrily and said, "This says he has to. If that anvil-headed jackass in there don't unbolt his damn door an' let us buy some likker right quick, I'm fixin' to throw him in a one-way ticket to hell."

"It's a bad idea," Billy said. "There's other places open in town."

The cowboy turned then, and for the first time spotted the city marshal's badge pinned to Billy's shirt. "Wal, looka here, boys," he drawled. "Junior's got hisself a bright shiny tin star on his chest, an' a mouthful of orders to go along with it. You must be some of that ass-kickin' law we been hearin' so much about in these parts."

"The name's Bill Bass an' I'm a deputy city marshal. Now you boys move along an' leave this man alone."

"Bill Bass, huh? Some of Wyatt Bass's people, are you?"

"His deputy an' his brother. But right now you don't need to worry 'bout that. All you have to worry 'bout is doin' what I told you to do."

"Else you'll go tell big brother, and he'll come over here an' spank our bee-hinds, huh?"

As the two men talked, Ridge began to watch the five other cowboys with increasing caution. They did not seem too happy about the prodding ways of their loud, boisterous companion, but Ridge guessed that if it came to a scrap, they would still back his play against Billy. They were preparing themselves for a fight as routinely as they might get ready to line out a herd for a river crossing. Ridge knew that the only thing that now stood between all of them and a sudden deadly shoot-out was whatever good sense and courage Billy Bass could muster, and the young deputy already stood facing an angry man who held a drawn revolver pointed at his belly.

Finally, ignoring the cowboy's companions as if they were no more threat than a crowd of strangers gathered to watch the confrontation, Billy stepped up close to his antagonist and looked him squarely in the eye, their faces no more than a foot apart.

"Is it worth a fight?" he asked earnestly. "You think about it a minute, an' if you decide it is, then let's get at it."

The cowboy continued to stare back at Billy and it seemed to Ridge that he could almost watch the man's mind working, weighing Billy's words and discovering the stark truth in them. There was no doubt that he could kill Billy in an instant simply by squeezing his trigger, but he seemed suddenly to realize what a foolish and shameful thing it would be to do that simply out of frustration at not being able to buy a drink.

At last, as a grin spread across his worn features, the tension seemed to melt away like ice on a hot griddle. As he holstered the drawn gun, he exclaimed, "I'll be danged if my big mouth don't get me in some of the goldangedest, most ignorant situations I ever seen a man wind up in. Ask the boys here if that ain't so."

A slight smile turned up the corners of Billy's mouth, then spread fully across his face. "It happens, cowboy," he said.

"So where's that open saloon you were talkin' about?" the cowboy asked.

"The Blue Eagle," Billy said, pointing over his shoulder with his thumb. "Two streets back, then turn north."

"Much obliged," the cowboy said. In a moment the whole troop had retrieved their horses and started away in the direction he indicated.

When Billy turned back to Ridge, his face was red and his eyes had an odd expression in them.

"Got a little tense there for a minute," Ridge drawled.

"I mean to tell you!" Billy said. "Hot damn, I was scared."

"Wal, Billy," Ridge grinned. "I can't rightly say that it showed."

"I sure was hopin' it wouldn't, Ridge. If he'd seen I was scared, it would have been all over with. But all the time we were standin' there, I just kept thinkin', 'Won't this be a stupid situation if we all start pullin' our guns an' blastin' away at each other just 'cause of a little puffed-up pride an' a bunch of tough talk?'"

"It would be at that," Ridge agreed. They walked on in silence for a moment, each feeling the built-up reservoirs of tension drain away inside them. Ridge finally said, "Tell me one thing, though, Billy."

"What's that?" Billy asked, casting a curious glance sideways at his companion.

"Tell me one more time how crazy it is for one lawman to go up against a bunch of tough, armed Texans jus' 'cause he thinks it's somethin' he has to do."

Billy did not answer, nor did he turn his head to

look over at Ridge again, but his eyes narrowed and his jaw set, and Ridge Parkman knew finally that he had at least one friend in town who knew why Ned Rakestraw had to be arrested.

CHAPTER FOUR

It was only his third day in Cornersville, and already the waiting and inactivity were beginning to strain Parkman's nerves. He had wired back to Kansas City, informing Captain Thomlinson of the two-week delay and suggesting that some other man might be sent to the town to relieve him. But a day later the discouraging three-word answer had come back. "Wait for Rakestraw."

So far only two people were supposed to know why Ridge Parkman was in town, but he was getting a funny feeling about that. Everywhere he went, it seemed that he was treated with unwarranted hostility and indifference. Only Billy Bass and Mabel Cain remained friendly to him, and the young deputy was busy much of the time so there was little opportunity to spend time in his company.

But Mabel had provided Ridge with some diversion from the long hours of sitting in saloons and wandering aimlessly around town. Since arriving in Cornersville, he had eaten every meal in her café, and she usually took the time to sit and chat with him awhile when he went in her place. On his second night in town he had stayed around the café until closing, and then had walked with her the few blocks to her simple frame home on the edge of town.

There was something about Mabel that appealed to Ridge, though he might have been hard put to decide exactly what it was. It certainly was not her looks, though after a time he did begin to find a certain attractiveness in her quick smile and her honest, straightforward gaze. It seemed to be more a matter of the way she looked at life, and the determined resilience with which she dealt with all the circumstances around her. She was strong, defiant, and ruggedly self-sufficient, and he admired those qualities in a woman.

If the situation was different, Ridge knew he could be having a good time here in Cornersville. There were saloons aplenty where a man could wash away a few accumulated weeks or months of trail dust, and his fingers were not completely unfamiliar with the feel of a deck of playing cards and a stack of chips. But he seldom indulged in such pleasures when there was business on hand. In an environment such as the one he found here in Cornersville, he knew he had to stay on his toes at every minute. Even two or three drinks could slow a man's draw just a fraction of a second, and that fraction might easily spell the difference between living and dying in a tight situation.

So he stayed sober and he stayed alert. Denver would still be there when the cell door slammed shut on Rakestraw.

It was midmorning, the time of day Parkman had grown the most fond of here in Cornersville. The blazing summer sun had yet to gather up its full, sweltering intensity, and the streets of the town were still rather peaceful and calm. He had just finished his leisurely breakfast at Mabel's and was strolling down the street toward where his horse was stabled. At least once a day he checked in on his faithful mount and friend, President Grant, and he had about decided that it was time to saddle up and take the animal out for some exercise.

He had gone about two blocks and had just passed the entrance to the Cattleman's Bank when an unfamiliar voice called out his name from behind. Ridge turned and saw a thin, mousey-looking little man standing in the doorway of the bank staring at him hesitantly.

"You are Marshal Parkman, aren't you?" the man asked.

"I use that handle most times," Ridge confirmed casually.

"Mr. Tackett told me if I was to see you this morning, I should ask you to step in a minute and talk to him."

"Mr. Tackett said that, huh?" Ridge asked. "I don't believe I know the gent."

"Why, he owns this bank, and he's also the mayor of Cornersville. He said he'd like to talk to you if it's convenient."

"I reckon it's convenient, all right," Ridge said.

The clerk led the way into the bank and across to a closed door at the back. When he knocked, a voice inside asked, "Who is it?"

"Crosby, sir," the clerk answered. "And I have Marshal Parkman with me."

The bank president met them at the door and introduced himself to Ridge with exaggerated cordiality. "Mr. Parkman, I'm Mike Tackett. I was told you were in town, and it's a great pleasure to meet you at last."

Then, turning to Crosby, he said, "Bob, please go take care of that errand we discussed earlier." In another instant the clerk was gone out the front door of the bank.

Ridge decided that there was something a little haywire about this setup. Tackett looked respectable and prosperous enough in his neat gray suit, white shirt, and starched collar, but there was something seedy and deceitful about his slightly crooked smile, and Ridge did not like the way his eyes worked overtime darting around the room like bee-stung hummingbirds. The man was nervous as hell about something, but he was doing his damnedest to cover it up.

"Please have a seat, Marshal," Tackett said, indicating the large, plush leather sofa which sat squarely in front of the great walnut desk that dominated the center of the room.

As Ridge slouched down easily into the chair, the banker went to a sideboard and said, "I'm told that my private stock of brandy is some of the best to be had this side of Kansas City. I have it shipped over from France and brought down by special courier from Missouri twice a year. Would you care to try some?"

"I reckon I better," Ridge drawled. "A man like me don't get much chance to drink that kind of liquor, so I better try some when I can." He accepted the glass the banker offered, sniffed it, and then waited for Tackett to take a sip first.

The brandy had a mild burn to it as it went down his throat, but it had a rich aroma and fruity flavor which he was not accustomed to from the common whiskey he usually bought in saloons. It was worth the stop just to sample this stuff.

"It's damn good," he told Tackett. "Much obliged."

"Perhaps I could persuade you to accept a bottle or two when you leave," the banker offered smoothly.

Ridge frowned slightly at that. A man just didn't go around giving away this kind of booze to strangers . . . at least not without some good reason. And the part of the remark about leaving did not slip by Parkman's notice either. Tackett only had four cards in the hole now. One was showing.

"I'd like the hell out of that," Ridge told him. "But the government don't allow it. Thanks jus' the same."

As Tackett moved around to his seat behind the desk, he said, "Tell me, Marshal. What's your impression of Cornersville so far?"

"You got yourself one ripsnortin' little town here, Mr. Tackett," Ridge said.

"Please. Make it Mike."

"Okay, Mike. An' Ridge'll do fine for me, too, since you want to go casual like. But now let me ask you one."

"Shoot."

"How come I'm sittin' here in this chair, pourin' down this high-toned brandy of yours? What can I do for you, Mike?"

Tackett leaned back in his chair, swirled his drink around in his glass, and smiled that evasive smile of his again. "You get right down to it, don't you, Ridge?" he asked.

"It's better that way sometimes," Parkman admitted.

"All right then," Tackett said. "I was hoping to wait for the others to get here, but since you asked . . ."

Just then there was another knock on the door and the banker went around with some relief to admit two other men into his office. The first was in his early forties, with a serious, scowling gaze that seemed to distrust the whole world around him. He wore a white cotton apron over his street clothes, and Tackett introduced him as Paul Kearney, owner of Kearney's General Merchandise and Supply, and an alderman on the Cornersville City Council.

The other man was dressed much as Tackett, in a neat business suit, starched shirt, and tie. His handshake was sweaty and flaccid, reminding Ridge of the feel of a dead fish. He was Henry Plumm, a lawyer and the city's attorney.

When they were all seated, Tackett told the two newcomers, "Gentlemen, Marshal Parkman prefers that we get right down to business, so Henry, if you would . . ."

Plumm took charge of the meeting, addressing Ridge in smooth, confidential tones which were apparently meant to inspire an air of confidence in him. Ridge was unimpressed and still on his guard.

"Marshal Parkman, Cornersville is a cattle town. We know it's rough here, and even dangerous sometimes, but we also know that without the cattle business which these Texas cowboys push up the trail every year, our town would dry up and blow off the map. And so with the unique realities that we have to deal with here, we've found over the years that it's better to make, uh, certain compromises, to fit the situation we find ourselves in."

"Dammit, Henry," the storekeeper, Kearney, interrupted sourly. "Why don't you just cut the crap and get right down to it. Nobody knows what you're talking about when you get into all that double-talking lawyer bullshit."

"I'm just trying to lay a little foundation for what we want to propose," Plumm said defensively.

"I got customers," Kearney griped. "I ain't got all day to sit around and flap my jaws like some I know."

With a resentful glance at his associate, Plumm turned back to Ridge, and this time he started getting nearer to the point. "Word has reached us about why you've come to our town, Marshal Parkman," he said. "And frankly, you have us all pretty worried. We don't quite know what will happen when you try to arrest Ned Rakestraw, but we know what could possibly happen, and it's pretty frightening."

"If it was just an ordinary cowboy," Tackett said, "that would be a different matter altogether. But a man like Ned Rakestraw . . . it could get real ugly."

"I don't like what I'm hearing," Ridge told them bluntly.

"It's not easy for any of us," Plumm told him. "But the problem is so grave that we felt it necessary to make this appeal to you."

"What appeal is that?"

"Don't arrest Ned Rakestraw in Cornersville," Tackett said. "It's as simple as that. We'd like you to leave town before you turn this whole place upside down. We know we can't order you out, and I doubt if even our city marshal could force you to leave without a battle, so we're hoping that we might be able to persuade you to go instead."

The banker paused a moment and glanced nervously at the others, as if to signal them what he was about to do. Then he plunged on. "Of course we know you must have had expenses in getting here, and there's been your room and board while you've been in town. We're prepared to provide some sort of restitution to you . . ."

"A thousand dollars, Parkman," Kearney interrupted impatiently. "You can have the cash this minute if you'll agree to pack up and be out of Cornersville today. We don't care where you go, or whether you wait ten miles down the road and put a bullet in Rakestraw as he rides out to go home. Just don't do it in Cornersville."

"That's clear enough," Ridge said. He let his eyes rove, meeting the glance of each of the other men, and then he said, "My answer is no."

"You don't have to decide this minute," Plumm cautioned. "We realize what a serious matter it is, attempting to influence such an obviously dedicated man as yourself but we are sincerely hoping that you will understand the serious predicament we find ourselves in."

"Don't be stupid, Marshal," Kearney said. "Take the money and git. It's more than you'd make in a year, and you can still trail him back to Texas and get him there. It's a sweet deal for you."

Ridge swirled the last swallow of brandy around in his glass and then shot it down his throat, savoring the warmth it radiated as it flowed down his throat. "You know, gentlemen," he said at last. "I been totin' a badge for right at fourteen years now, an' in all that time I've got some crazy notions built up in my head 'bout the job I do. One of them is that you can't stand up for the law sometimes, an' other times let things slip by you, not an' still hold your head up an' feel good about callin' yourself a lawman.

"You set this up real sweet, an' all four of us know I can't arrest you 'cause there's no witnesses to tell how you tried to bribe me. But I can warn you to stay out of my business. You'll regret it if you don't."

"You're stupid, Parkman."

"Mebbe so," Ridge answered. He could feel a sort of cold anger building up inside him and struggled to keep it in check. He rose to his feet, hitched up his gunbelt, and tucked the back of his shirttail in, forcing himself to calm the fury which threatened to explode into violence.

The storekeeper rose, too, and was about to speak again, but Ridge reached out impulsively, grabbing himself a handful of shirt and white apron, and pulled Kearney over close to him. "If I was you," he said in a low tone that scarcely concealed his rage, "I'd give some serious thought to keepin' my trap shut for a while." Then he gave the man a quick shove, which landed him clumsily back in the chair he had just left.

"I ain't out to hurt this damn town of yours, nor nobody in it," Parkman told them. "I'd about as soon be any other place you can name, but the fact is I'm here, an' Ned Rakestraw's on his way, an' I'm takin' him in. Don't cross me!"

None of the three of them said another word as he marched to the door and stormed out of the bank.

Once he hit the street, Parkman took off at a quick pace, headed for the stable and his horse. He figured he'd better get away from this town and everybody in it for a while, because the way he felt at the moment, the next person who happened to look crossways at him might end up getting carried to the doctor.

CHAPTER FIVE

Wyatt Bass was leaned back in his chair with his feet up on the edge of the dining table, picking his teeth with the slim, silver toothpick that the grateful citizenry of Salinas had given him when he decided to move on to greener and more violent pastures. The room was large and elaborately decorated according to the expensive tastes of the marshal. The walls were paneled with shiny imported mahogany, and a large, crystal chandelier was suspended from the ceiling directly over the heavy mahogany table, which was the main fixture of the room. The table doubled as a dining table when Bass decided to eat in and entertain friends, and as a poker table when he put together one of his legendary, marathon high-stakes poker games.

It was his favorite place, and one of the first rooms to be outfitted and decorated when Bass purchased this building and set up his Dixie Darling Saloon. People in town knew it as Wyatt's Office, though he also had a separate city marshal's office down the street, and to be invited into the fellowship of this place was generally considered to be a high honor in Cornersville.

The usual crowd was there at the moment. Felicia,

his current lady, sat on his left, picking daintily at the remnants of a baked trout, which lay staring back up at her from her plate. She was a slim, curvaceous beauty whose dancing dark eyes and shimmering cascades of black hair indicated a strong strain of Spanish aristocracy in her background. Though noon was more than an hour past, she still wore the silky yellow dressing gown that she had put on when they got up that morning.

To the marshal's left was Paul Halliday, Bass's best friend, the head dealer in the casino section of the Dixie Darling, and half owner of the entire operation. He was a husky man of medium height, with the slick charm and good looks of a riverboat gambler or a successful pimp. Though little about his outward appearance pointed to the fact, he was an explosively dangerous man and a veritable walking artillery barrage. The armory which he carried almost constantly on his person included cut-down twin Colts in shoulder holsters under each arm, a tiny revolver inside his left boot, a spring-loaded derringer along his right forearm, and a six-inch, flip-blade knife in a special sheath under his coat in the small of his back.

Along one side of the table sat Joseph Gulick, a spectacled, aging little man who would have looked quite in place behind the desk in a library, or wearing a green eyeshade bent over the ledgers in an accountant's office. He was owner of the largest firearms store in Cornersville, a master craftsman in the custom manufacture of guns, and Bass's personal armorer for the past eight years.

Matt Rikard, head bartender and manager of the Dixie Darling, sat facing Gulick, already working on his fourth glass of straight rye whiskey. Rikard had the veined red face and constant bleary-eyed expression of a dedicated drinker, but he did a good job and kept the employees from stealing the business blind, so the marshal tolerated his alcoholism with quiet disdain.

There were two other women at the table, too, saloon girls from the Dixie Darling that Bass had brought in as companions for his friends.

During the meal the men had been discussing business. Halliday and Rikard had presented the accounts from their separate areas of responsibility, and then the four of them had begun to consider the possibility of Bass purchasing a second saloon across the tracks on the south side. Bass would soon be closing a place down there because its owner refused to quit poisoning his customers with inferior, bootleg whiskey, and when that happened, the building and fixtures would be available at a bargain price.

But after the meal, as the Mexican maid was clearing away the plates and glasses from the big table, Wyatt Bass lapsed into one of his favorite pastimes when he was in intimate company such as this. He was spinning yarns about his adventures as a lawman.

His audience waited while he probed with the silver toothpick for a small morsel of steak wedged in between two of his front teeth. He had a knack for such dramatic pauses, leaving his listeners hanging for an instant or two before plunging on and explaining how he got himself out of some dangerous situation or other.

Finally he said, "I knew ol' Rip and the other two were in the cabin, 'cause I'd already spotted their horses where they left them in a little grove down by the creek. But I knew I didn't have a chance in hell of goin' in there by myself an' blastin' them out.

"But I had to do somethin' pretty quick, 'cause I still thought the rest of Rip's gang was on their way to rendezvous with him at this cabin."

"Yeah, you didn't know we'd already surrounded the rest of 'em an' gunned two of 'em down in Paiute Canyon," Halliday chuckled. "That's just like you, Wyatt. Gettin' ready to storm in there an' take the whole bunch like Sherman took Atlanta, rather than back off a bit an' look for some help."

"Hell, Paul," Bass exclaimed. "I knew I finally had ol' Rip Baker by the short hairs, an' I wasn't about to let him go. Not on your life." He paused again to carefully insert the toothpick in the vest pocket of his white linen dress coat, then picked up a cigar from an ashtray in front of him and relit it. "If I can't go in after them, I thought, then I'll have to make them come out to me. I studied on the problem for a minute, an' I decided that the best way to make a man leave a building you don't want him in is to burn it down on top of him. Then I remembered them two little shells Joe give me some time before. He said when he give them to me that they'd start fires, but I didn't see much use for them at the time, so I just stuck them in the back loops of my pistol belt."

"Phosphorus," the little gunsmith explained. "The Army experimented with it back during the war, but I was the first to develop a model that ignites on impact instead of during trajectory."

"I didn't know what the hell they were going to do," Bass said, cutting short the technical explanation impatiently, so he could get on with the tale. "But Joe hadn't never let me down before, so I figgered it was worth a try. I put the first one through a front window, but they got the fire out before a blaze caught hold. Then I played it safe an' popped the other one into the roof where they couldn't get at the fire.

"Man, you never seen anything like it. That little shack went up like a tinderbox. It couldn't of been more'n five minutes, when out comes Rip, blastin' away like a maniac in the dark, an' tryin' to make a break for the horses. I was waitin' for him behind a stump about twenty yards away, an' with the fire behind him it was like shootin' ducks in a barrel. I took my time an' put him away with one bullet right here." Bass's right index finger came up and he tapped himself between the eyes.

"When the second one came out, Duke Smith I think it was, I dropped him right in the door an' he fell back in the cabin. I never did see no sight of the third one. He must of burnt up, 'cause in another minute that whole place came down in one big roarin' pile. It was a sight."

"That's some story, Wyatt, honey," Felicia said. Bass glanced over at her and felt a little surge of pleasure at the way her dark eyes were studying him with admiration and respect.

"It was a shore 'nough bad day for the Rip Baker Gang the day they decided to take the Bank of Salinas," Bass said. "When I got back to town, Paul an' the rest of the posse had the last three already in jail, an' three days later we strung up the lot of 'em right in the middle of court square."

"Yeah, the hangin' drew a crowd from thirty miles around," Halliday added. "It was the first triple hangin' they'd had in nine years, an' a week later the town council doubled Wyatt's salary."

"Town folks love a good hangin'," Bass agreed. "If you hang an owlhoot for a town now'n again, there ain't nothin' you can't have from that town if you want it."

"I went to a hanging once down in Lubbock," Felicia said. "It was so horrible it gave me chilblains all over, but I remember I couldn't take my eyes off that man's feet danglin' around in the air like they did. It just fascinated me somehow."

Bass looked over and grinned at her, patting her thigh familiarly through the soft material of her gown. "It's a funny thing 'bout hangings," he said. "You'd think it would be somethin' you couldn't drag a woman to, but it's the females that like 'em the best. They always come by the dozens to watch."

Bass and Felicia had been together nearly a month now. Matt had hired her as one of the saloon hostesses, but she had remained on the line only three days before Bass chose her as his new favorite. During the day she was an attentive, kittenish companion, but at night she was an insatiable hellcat. Bass had the feeling that the two of them would stay together much longer than usual.

A knock sounded at the door behind Matt, and a moment later the bartender on duty opened the door and stuck his head in hesitantly.

Matt turned in his chair and asked, "Yeah, Ernie? What is it?"

"There's a fella out here," Ernie said with a frown. "He's . . . uh . . ." He glanced over at Bass with a confused expression on his face.

"Spit it out, man," Matt snapped impatiently. "You got a troublemaker out there?"

"No, it's not that," Ernie said. "But he said he was going to arrest me if I didn't let him in to see Marshal Bass. I told him you were busy, but he really acts like he means what he says. He calls himself Parkman."

"That damn Parkman!" Bass exclaimed with disgust. "Matt, you go out an' make him wait awhile before you bring him back. Tell him if he wants to talk to me, he'll have to wait 'til I get damn good an' ready to see him."

When the bartender was gone, Bass turned to the others and said, "Everybody out except Paul. Leave by the back door. Felicia, I guess you can stay, too, but sit over there an' keep your trap shut." The girl followed his orders, getting up and moving to a nearby couch without comment.

Finally Bass turned to Halliday and said, "We gotta do somethin' about this son of a bitch, Paul. That's all there is to it."

"I know, Wyatt," Halliday said. "But since he's a federal man, it won't be no easy thing. I haven't ever heard of this Ridge Parkman before he came here, but one look at him an' you can tell he's got grit."

"We gotta do somethin'," Bass repeated insistently. "I've been talking to the mayor an' some of the businessmen around town, an' they think like I do. A thing like this might make some of the big Texas outfits start lookin' toward some other market towns for their beeves. Colorado's prime to steal the trade from us, an' then we'd really be out in the rain with no slicker. I can't exactly order a U.S. Marshal out of town like a rowdy cowboy, but he's gotta be stopped some way before Rakestraw hits town with his crew."

"There's ways, Wyatt," Halliday said ominously. "You an' I both know he can be stopped if it comes right down to the line."

"I'd hate to think it would come to that," Bass said, glancing over at Felicia nervously to see if she was paying any attention to the conversation. His lovely young mistress was cleaning the dirt from under her toenails with one long, slender fingernail.

"Nobody'd like it," Halliday said, "but if it came right down to the line an' he still wouldn't give . . ."

"If it comes to that, I don't want to know a thing 'til it's all over, Paul. You'd have to pick this one up an' go with it all on your own."

"I got you, Wyatt," Halliday said.

Wyatt Bass and Paul Halliday had been together for more than ten years now as business associates and the closest of friends, and the union had always been comfortable and profitable for both of them. Their first encounter had been back in Salinas in a casino where Wyatt had worked part-time as a faro dealer under Halliday, who had been in charge of the gaming tables. Within a year, the two men had pooled their resources and bought the casino they worked in.

The two had thrived as partners, and when Bass made the move to Cornersville, there was never any question that Paul Halliday would come along to manage the business side of whatever enterprises they decided to set up there.

Wyatt Bass liked being a peace officer. He liked the image and prestige that went with the wearing of a badge, and he literally craved the danger and excitement that was such an integral part of being a lawman. But he was a man who liked his comforts, too, and early in his career he realized that a man was never going to accumulate much wealth nor live in style on the slim salaries which most communities paid the men who protected their lives and properties.

So he had diversified, and finally with the aid of Halliday, and in the ideal surroundings of a place like

Cornersville, he was able to attain the best of both worlds. It was Bass's name and presence that kept the crowds jamming the Dixie Darling, but it was Halliday's shrewd, behind-the-scenes management that had turned it into the lucrative property that it now was.

But in the simple appearance of such an unimpressive figure as Ridge Parkman, Bass was beginning to get the uneasy feeling that the foundations of his continued prosperity here were being threatened. On the one hand, he was a sworn officer of the law, a responsibility which he took quite seriously in his own way. He knew he should help Parkman. Yet on the other hand, he knew that if he helped out with the arrest of Ned Rakestraw, which very likely might result in the killing and wounding of several of the Circle Bar G crew, such an act would do irreparable damage to the goodwill which Cornersville had taken years to build up with the Texas ranchers and trail hands. And because his personal finances had become so intertwined with the prosperity of the town, what was bad for Cornersville would be bad for Wyatt Bass.

It was a dilemma that he had yet to see his way clear of, but in the last couple of days he had been feeling an ever increasing resentment toward this newcomer, this Ridge Parkman, for placing him in such a discomforting and threatening position.

In a few minutes the door opened and Matt stepped back to admit the federal marshal. Parkman stopped in the doorway and surveyed the room in a calm, cautious manner before coming on in. But even that simple gesture told Bass a lot. *So it's come to this already,* the city marshal thought. *Here we are, two sworn lawmen, and we trust each other as much as either of us would trust a coiled rattlesnake.*

After determining that there were no hidden dangers to him in the room, Parkman took another moment to survey the lavish fixtures in the place, allowing his eyes to linger over the lovely Felicia with a particularly appreciative glance.

"You've got a real fine layout here, Marshal," Parkman said, letting a slight smile move across his face. "All the comforts." Bass studied his features for a moment, but could form no impression of what sort of mood he might be in. This Parkman was a cool one all right. He might look like nothing more than a slouchy cowhand in his faded jeans, wrinkled shirt, scruffy boots, and dusty hat, but there was a lot more beneath his surface than might be apparent on first glance. He was a man to be handled cautiously.

"I do all right," Bass said. "The State of Kansas has never passed a law that says just because a man pins on a badge, he has to live like a hard-luck steer jockey."

Parkman just grinned and said nothing. His eyes began to roam around the room again, taking in the well-stocked liquor shelf, the fine china and silver service on the sideboard, Bass's immaculate white suit, and again, the beautiful Felicia. Now that he was in, he seemed in no particular hurry to get to whatever business he had come here to discuss. *Damn you, Parkman,* Bass thought. *Get on with it or get out.*

"Sorry to keep you waiting out there, Marshal," Bass said, "but I was discussing business with my friend here. Ridge Parkman, this is Paul Halliday." The two exchanged nods of greeting, but when Parkman spoke again, his words were aimed at Bass.

"No problem," he said. "Mostly I've jus' been waitin' 'round town anyway. Might as well do it in your saloon as anyplace else." Again he fell silent, and again Bass waited a tense moment before speaking up again.

"So, what do you need?" he asked finally.

Parkman looked down at the chair in front of him as if noticing it for the first time. Pointing to it, he asked, "Do you mind?"

"Sure. Have a seat."

Parkman dropped down into the chair, shifted a little to get more comfortable, and then looked up at Bass. Their eyes met squarely across the eight feet which separated, and in an instant Bass saw all traces of good-humor and friendliness drain from Parkman's expression.

"I jus' met your mayor this morning," Parkman said, "an' I come within about an inch of rearrangin' his face for him."

"I'm glad you didn't," Bass said.

"Wal, when I thought about it awhile, I decided that if anybody in this town needs their ass kicked, it isn't him . . . it's you." The statement was made in such a calm, deliberate tone that for an instant Bass just stared back, scarcely able to believe what he had just heard. To his right, Paul Halliday had raised his arm up casually—one quick, downward flip and the derringer would be in his palm, ready to be fired. Parkman raised his left hand, pointed one finger at Halliday, and said, "Don't!" The one-word command was heavy with unmistakable threat of death, and on a sign from Bass, Halliday slowly lowered his arm back down to the tabletop.

The three of them sat in silence for a moment, letting the threat of an impending shoot-out drain slowly away. Then finally Parkman went on, and though his voice remained calm, Bass could sense that here was a man who had taken all the aggravation he intended to take.

"Things could have been a helluva lot different between you an' me, Bass," he said, "but wishin' don't put the eggs back in the basket. So here's how it's gonna be. First, I'm takin' Ned Rakestraw when he hits town, an' anybody that tries to stop me's got two choices. Die or go to jail. I coulda used your help with the arrest, but now I wouldn't trust you even if you offered. You don't strike me as bein' a very reliable man, no matter what the storytellers might say 'bout you."

Bass's eyes burned at the harshness of the insult, but he remained silent, teeth gritted, as Parkman went on.

"Second," Parkman went on. "From here on, I'm stayin' out of your way, an' you're stayin' the hell out of mine. It seems like that's the only arrangement that'll keep both of us alive 'til I can do my job an' get the hell out of Cornersville.

"Marshal, you're a man with a whale of reputation with a gun, an' I don't doubt for a second that you've earned every line of it the hard way. I've seen you draw, an' I know you're as fast as the business end of a bullwacker's whip. But that don't mean you can't be beat. You an' I both know that there ain't a gunhand alive so fast that he won't get beat one time or 'nother by somebody. It ain't no threat to tell you that if the day comes when you an' I have to tangle, you might have one whale of a surprise comin' at you.

"This is your town, Bass. You took it fair an' square from the rowdies that had it 'fore you come. But Cornersville's still in the Union, too, an' that puts it in my bailiwick. Long as you don't forget that, we'll be fine. If you do, an' if you cross me, I'll lock you up in your own jail 'til I can get you to a federal court for trial."

Bass could feel the muscles in his shoulders knotting with tension because of the fury he was holding inside. It took every fiber of self-control he possessed to resist the urge to leap up immediately and put an end to this ridiculous situation once and for all. Parkman seemed to be making no visible preparations to defend himself, and Bass knew that he and Halliday could easily win the fight. But the time and the place weren't right.

With deliberate calm, Parkman rose from his chair and pushed it back neatly under the table as he had found it. He afforded Halliday a curt nod, then turned to Felicia and made a more courteous gesture of farewell, smiling slightly and mumbling, "Ma'am."

Bass's strong thick fingers gripped the arms of his chair until his knuckles turned white. It had been many years since any man had found the audacity to speak to him like that, and even longer since he had permitted it to happen without action. But he knew that even if he did draw on Parkman and killed him here, it would be sheer lunacy. Killing a federal marshal here in the back room of his own saloon could only bring endless trouble.

It was a new and utterly frustrating feeling to have to just sit there and take it, but he did take it, not knowing what else to do at the moment. He would get a chance later, though. Of that he was sure. Somehow he always got even.

Parkman turned and left the room without further comment, closing the door easily behind him. The three of them sat silently in the room a moment longer, then Halliday tried to say something. "Wyatt, I don't . . ." he began.

"Shut up, Paul," Bass said.

"But I was just going to say . . ."

"I said shut up . . . and get out!" Bass hissed. His tone left no doubt that he meant it, and Halliday quickly rose and left the room, not wanting to risk receiving the brunt of Bass's stored up fury.

"You, too," Bass told Felicia. "Get your ass out of here, woman."

Felicia, looking half insulted and half frightened, left the room, moving through the back doorway to the saloon girls' living quarters with a defiant swish of silks.

When everybody else was gone, Wyatt Emerson Bass sat for a long time, staring at the closed door in front of him, toying with the grips of his twin revolvers, and thinking vengeful thoughts.

CHAPTER SIX

The Cornersville Opera House, built to handle a capacity crowd of about four hundred, was packed with nearly seven hundred men and women, all jamming every available seat as well as the aisles, orchestra pit, cloak rooms, and foyer. The din in the place was overwhelming, and though smoking was not permitted for obvious reasons in the wooden building, bottles circulated freely and the crowd was in tremendously high spirits. Everybody had plenty of time to get that way, because most of them had found their places two and three hours earlier to insure that they would be on hand to see this memorable show.

Eddie Ray was practically an institution in the culturally deprived and entertainment-hungry little western towns such as Cornersville. He was a one-man show who traveled the western regions, from the largest cities to the rudest mining camps and settlements, performing his repertory of songs, dance, theatrical sketches, and comedy.

For the past couple of days wave after wave of excitement had swept through the town because of Ray's upcoming appearance. The energy levels that were stirred up easily rivaled the time when Wyatt Bass had organized a forty-three-member posse to go out and

hunt down the Easy River Gang, or the day when
Judge Bradshaw had scheduled the multiple hangings
of the five surviving gang members.

The opera house was the pride and joy of the dozen
or so local merchants who had pooled their funds to
have it built. An architect had been imported all the
way from New York City to supervise its design and
construction, and few expenses had been spared to
make it one of the most ornate and gaudy entertainment palaces in the state. But most of the cultural em-
bellishments were wasted on the hordes of dirty, rowdy
Texas cowboys who crowded the place this evening.
They just wanted to see a good show, and when the
scheduled time of eight o'clock arrived and the her-
alded performer had not yet made his appearance, tem-
pers began to rise. A lot of embittered comments began
to float around the packed, steamy hall about what
might happen to the opera palace and the entire town
of Cornersville if Ray did not show up in short order.

Ridge Parkman had found a seat in the back of the
hall atop a cabinet that was high enough for him to
have a clear view over the heads of the people seated
between him and the stage. From where he sat, he
spotted Marshal Bass in the cluster of seats reserved
near the front for the prominent citizens of the town.

Since his confrontation with Bass a few days before,
Ridge had been able to stay clear of the city marshal,
as he had hoped. He was pleased by how calmly the
days had passed and now saw the possibility that he
could go ahead and apprehend his prisoner without
ever having to exchange another word with the city
marshal. But the antagonism that existed between him
and Wyatt Bass had not affected the friendship which
he was forming with the young deputy, Billy Bass.

The differences between the two marshals had placed Billy in a difficult position. On the one hand, he seemed to respect Ridge Parkman and the mission he had come here to do. He even had a personal liking for the visiting federal marshal. But he was also a great supporter and protégé of his brother, seeming at times to be the total captive of Wyatt Bass's dominant personality and overpowering will.

Parkman returned the friendship to the young deputy, glad to have an ally in this hostile place, and recognizing in Billy the same strong respect for the law and the desire to see it upheld that Ridge himself felt. But he had no desire to drive a wedge between the two brothers, nor to destroy the admiration Billy felt for Wyatt. Long after he was gone, these two men were going to have to live with each other and work side by side.

As eight thirty came and passed, it seemed at times as if the crowd might literally explode in a fit of temper at having to wait so long in these hot, crowded surroundings without a sign of the entertainer. Finally, at one point, it seemed that the fuse for the expected trouble had been lit.

Somewhere near the center of the ocean of humanity a cowboy stood up on his seat and began to shout, his deep voice sounding out over the general uproar in the place.

"Bring on the show," he bellowed, weaving drunkenly as he struggled to stay atop his chair until he had his say. "Either we see Eddie Ray step on that stage pretty quick, or a bunch of us good ol' Texas boys are a'goin to turn this gussied-up cow palace into a pile of kindling an' cart it back to the Lone Star State for our winter's wood."

Drunken cowboys all around him began to shout out their agreement that maybe the destruction of the opera palace might be a good expression of their anger at not being properly entertained.

Wyatt Bass, on a front row seat with Felicia on one side of him and Mayor Tackett on the other, permitted the threats of violence to go on only for a moment. Just as the rabble-rousing cowboy was gathering his bravado for a second series of destructive suggestions, Bass rose to his feet.

As Ridge watched from a distance, it seemed to him that Bass almost formally excused himself from his companions before turning to deal with the trouble at hand. When he started to move back across the hall, as had happened before in the saloon, a path seemed to part magically in front of him. He made his way up the aisle with deliberate calm, then started down the row of seats toward the shouting cowboy. The level of noise and shouting in the place decreased noticeably as hundreds of pairs of eyes watched Bass move toward the troublemaker who was suggesting the destruction of a town landmark.

The cowboy calmed down considerably when he saw Bass coming, apparently deciding to explain his actions rather than forcing a confrontation. But Bass was not interested in hearing anything the man had to say. With movements which were at once smooth and yet amazingly fast, the marshal pushed back the tail of his long black suitcoat, drew his left revolver, and gave the cowboy a smack alongside his head that sounded with a meaty *thwack* all over the stunned opera palace. The cowboy went over like a felled tree into the waiting hands of his subdued supporters.

Pointing to a window on the side of the building,

Bass said something to the men around him. Then the unconscious body of the cowboy was hoisted aloft and began a bizarre, hand-over-hand journey above the heads of the crowd. When he finally arrived at the window, the men nearest to it pitched him unceremoniously out of the opening.

With that chore finished, Bass turned and made his way back down to his seat in the front row. Surprisingly, as he parted the tails of his coat and sat back down, the laughter and enjoyment the men in the hall felt at this little show turned into a spontaneous cheer, which Bass did not acknowledge with even a sideways glance.

And then, slowly, the intensity of the noise in the place faded as the realization moved back through the crowd that music was beginning down front.

When Eddie Ray appeared on stage, he was a bundle of dancing, singing energy. He was dressed in an outlandish gray-and-yellow striped suit which was a size or more too large for his lanky frame. On his head he wore a gray derby, and he carried a black cane, which he twirled and tossed during his routine with practiced ease. Momentarily the music, as well as the words of the song he sang, were lost in the tumultuous uproar of the crowd. But finally the jubilant audience quieted as Ray gained their rapt attention.

The song was a bawdy and fast-paced number about a girl called Goosey Goosey Lucy, the Terror of Patoosie, and the crowd loved it.

When the tune had ended, Ray strode to the center of the stage, staring out over the audience with an exaggerated frown on his face, and exclaimed, "I hate playing to an empty house! It seems like if I had the good graces to come all this way to bring some culture to you yokels, the least you could do would be to get a decent crowd together to see me!"

That led into a comedy routine specifically tailored for this area. In it he managed to make fun of the state of Kansas, Cornersville, and a host of local politicians, businessmen, and prominent figures, always treading the fine line between insult and comedy.

Next followed a skit that brought Ridge a particularly perverse satisfaction. With the aid of several locals for his straight men, Ray portrayed a bumbling incompetent marshal who was convinced that he was the hottest thing to wear a badge since Wild Bill Hickock. Before the piece was finished, he had succeeded in executing about half the citizens of his make-believe town and had let the bank robbers escape right under his nose. At the great distance that separated them, Ridge could not see what effect the skit had on Wyatt Bass, but he could imagine.

The show went well. For two solid hours Ray was a whirlwind of unbridled energy, keeping his audience enthralled with his wide variety of talented performances. But the high point of the evening came unexpectedly during one of the final comedy routines that Ray had planned for the evening.

All night the Texas cowboys had laughed uproariously during the skits and monologues that made fun of practically everybody and everything in Cornersville, but their senses of humor began to dull rapidly when at last Ray began unleashing his venomous brand of humor at them in particular. As he began the routine, they accepted the first few jabs good-naturedly, receiving the jokes about bowed legs, bad odors, and cow piles with at least courteous appreciation. But at last Ray, either through ignorance or defiance, stepped onto a piece of sacred ground which the cowboys could not tolerate.

It happened during a piece about a cowboy named Frank and his horse named Bob. Frank and Bob were far out on the range and had apparently been there for some time, judging from Frank's frame of mind. The cowboy was telling his horse how lonely it got out like that, away from women and liquor and all the pleasures of town. It was all acceptable enough to the Texans, but as the skit progressed and it became more apparent how Frank proposed to deal with his loneliness at Bob's expense, that was more than they could stand.

Ray was so intently into his performance that for a moment he did not notice the immediate shift in the tone of his audience from jovial to ugly. But it did not take the cowboys long to catch his attention and get their message across to him.

From somewhere back a few rows from the stage a cowboy rose to his feet and twirled a rope gracefully in the air a couple of times before releasing one end of it. The loop sailed through the air and settled gently over Ray's head, drawing tight around his arms and chest as the cowboy tugged on the free end. As Ray stumbled sideways and fell to the stage, pandemonium broke loose in the hall. Immediately a dozen or more cowboys were on the stage, scrambling for the privilege of hog-tying Ray like a calf and hauling him aloft.

As if by prearranged agreement, his wriggling form passed down from the stage, across the orchestra pit, and into the waiting hands of dozens of men who were ready to send him on toward the rear door of the hall.

Ridge watched the whole process with an amused smile on his face. Whatever they concocted to do to him outside, Ray was in for a rough time now, but Ridge doubted that any of the cowboys actually meant the entertainer any serious harm. They were just a bunch of rough men who lived and played hard, and Ridge thought that Ray should have taken that into consideration before he made the kind of jokes he did. Eddie Ray was no newcomer to the West, no greenhorn who might be forgiven for an occasional transgression out of ignorance, and in Ridge's mind, he had brought all of this on himself by affronting the particularly close relationship between a man and his horse.

As the packed crowd in the opera hall poured out into the street, Ridge moved along with the flow of humanity, as curious as any of the others about what the ringleaders might dream up to inflict on the hapless Eddie Ray.

By the time he got outside, several men had already torn a hitching rail down from in front of Kearney's General Merchandise and were in the process of tying it onto the rear of a jittery cow pony that had been appropriated from nearby. Then, when Ray was suitably tied straddling the rail, a cowboy jumped astride the horse and started away at a gallop. The crowd loved it, and their uproarious jeering and laughter only served to spur the terrified pony on to greater speeds.

Horse, rider, and unwilling passenger made two speedy rounds in a circle around the nearby railroad depot, treating Ray to several teeth-rattling jolts each time they bounced across the railroad tracks. Finally the cowboy brought the horse to a halt again in the midst of the crowd in front of the opera house.

As several of the men were releasing Ray from the rail, shouts began to go up for other escapades the comedian might be treated to. Finally, the voices of several men began to rise in unison, shouting "Wet 'im down!", and everybody began to agree that a dip in the town well, just west of the depot, was just what Eddie Ray needed. But the entertainer's spirits were never daunted. Throughout the entire humiliating experience he kept up a frantic monologue, subjecting his tormentors to an imaginative flood of insults and curses.

As the cowboys carried Ray to the well and began to tie the rope around his ankles, Ridge started looking around the crowd with increasing apprehension, trying to spot either of the Bass brothers to make sure they were monitoring all of this in case it did begin to get out of hand.

Finally he spotted Wyatt Bass, standing on the board sidewalk in front of the opera house with Felicia on his arm, staring out over the crowd like a benevolent father watching the youthful high jinks of his exuberant brood. He had a broad grin on his face and did not seem in the least inclined to stop the merriment, but at least Ridge was reassured by the fact that he was still there to put a stop to things if they did begin to go too far.

When the rope was secured around the entertainer's ankles, he was hauled off the ground and passed head first down the well, then one particularly burly Texan began to turn the heavy crank to lower him down to the water. Above the shouts and laughter of the crowd, Ray's defiant voice could be heard, echoing hauntingly up from the depths of the well like a voice from another world and taunting his persecutors. The length of his dips in the water could be measured only by the interruptions of his cursing, and after a dozen or so such interludes, the big cowboy began to haul him up to the top again.

As Ray was set upright and two men began to loosen the rope from his ankles, he sputtered, blew a flood of water from his nose, and gasped out, "Is it true that Texans get to smelling so bad sometimes that the cows demand to sleep upwind from them?"

New threats and suggestions began to rise up from the crowd around him, but Ray's voice could still be heard above the rest. "I heard that Texans are around cows so much that they make their wives bleat at night, so they'll feel more comfortable around them."

"Up the flagpole!" somebody shouted, and in a moment he was being hauled away toward the towering staff which rose more than forty feet in the air in front of the Cornersville Post Office. This time as two men were tying his feet together to haul him up, two more began to bind his hands behind him. Then, almost as an afterthought, a filthy neckerchief from around some man's throat was stuffed into the comedian's mouth and secured there by a piece of rope around his head. At least the taunts were silenced.

He was hauled aloft by three men, and then the lower end of the rope was tied off, and he was allowed to remain there for several minutes, never struggling as he swayed slightly against the pole. A couple of shots were fired, but the members of the crowd put a quick stop to that. Nobody actually wanted to hurt Eddie Ray. They just wanted to have a little fun with him in their own rough way.

When at last he was lowered to the ground and his limbs freed, the entertainer displayed a broad, if somewhat disheveled grin, and said, "I guess I've had enough if you men have. In all this crowd do you suppose there might be one swallow of good whiskey for a poor, loud-mouthed song-and-dance man from Albany, or have you Texans swilled up every drop of it already?"

Immediately a dozen bottles were offered, and Ray, taking ahold of one of them by the neck, tipped it back and downed about a third of its contents. "Ah, sweet salve that soothes the wounds of life's misfortunes," he proclaimed. "By God, for another jolt of that stuff I'd almost be willing to take another dive down that well over there."

But there was no need, because by then there was more whiskey being offered to him than he could drink in a week. As he accepted another bottle and sampled its contents, somebody shouted from the crowd, "An' what's your opinion of Texans now, Mister Ray?"

"Damned if it doesn't seem smarter to be with you than against you," the entertainer shouted.

"But there's some around yet as wouldn't agree with that," a hostile male voice said from somewhere nearby.

Ridge glanced around and saw that the speaker was no more than four feet from him and was staring straight at him. For an instant, he was not sure that the comment had been directed at him, but a moment later his worst fears were confirmed.

"We got us a man here what thinks he's gotta arrest a honest, hard-workin' Texas poke an' haul him off to the gallows for killin' a man in a fair fight."

Belatedly Ridge rebuked himself for being caught out in the middle of the crowd like this. While the activity had centered on Eddie Ray, he had been nothing more than another anonymous body in the crowd, but now, suddenly, he had been identified and was the center of attention to dozens of men who had nothing but hostile feelings toward him. It was a mistake that he realized could be fatal to him.

"Mebbe we should jus' go ahead on an' take care of one more loud-mouthed smart aleck 'fore we stop this here party," Ridge's antagonist suggested.

But Ridge remained indecisive for only an instant before beginning the only course of action which might get him out of this dangerous situation. Concentrating all his attention on the one man who was threatening him, he said, "I'm here an' ready as hell if you'd like to go ahead an' try it."

He had hoped that if he could turn it into a one-to-one confrontation with his accuser, the remainder of the crowd might be satisfied to just stand back and let the two of them fight it out. But at the moment all the Texans were geared to mob action and would not be content to stay out of it.

"Get his gun!" somebody called out, and immediately a dozen hands took ahold of Ridge and restrained him before he had a chance to defend himself.

Seeing his opponent so suddenly restrained, the cowboy who had first identified Ridge felt a new surge of bravado. "Boys," he shouted. "What should we do with an hombre that goes around hangin' Texans for no good cause?"

The suggestions which arose were very different from the harmless pranks that had been imposed on Eddie Ray. The sense of frivolity and good fun was draining quickly from the crowd and was replaced by an ugly mood of vengeance.

"Hang 'im like he wants to do to Rakestraw," one man shouted out.

"Tar an' feathers!"

"Drag 'im through the cactus!"

As Parkman struggled with his captors, hoping to at least free one of his arms for a moment so he could take a swing at somebody, anybody, his eyes darted to the spot in front of the opera palace where Wyatt Bass had been standing a few moments before. Now the city marshal was nowhere in sight. Ridge realized suddenly that he was completely on his own and that he could not count on Bass's aid even in this desperate situation.

"Ain't you man enough to face me one-to-one?" Ridge hissed, taunting his main persecutor.

"We Texans stand together in things like this," the man answered. There seemed to be a trace of relief in his voice because he had the support of all those around him and did not have to face the furious lawman on his own.

"Then you stand against the law," Ridge warned.

"So be it, Marshal. We do what we gotta do to protect our own."

The same rope, which had minutes before bound Eddie Ray's hands at the flagpole, was now tied around Ridge Parkman's hands, and across the way he could see two men fashioning the loose end of the flagpole rope into a slip knot. He struggled again in a frenzied burst of energy, but the stout men from Texas held him fast.

Then there was a sudden confused commotion off at the edge of the crowd to the left. Everybody turned to see what was going on, and in a moment Billy Bass came pushing his way roughly through the crowd to where Ridge was being held.

He already had his pistol in his hand, and when he

reached Ridge, he pointed it in the general direction of the men who held him and said, "You ain't doin' this."

"Go on, Billy," one of the men told him angrily. "You don't see your brother shovin' in here tryin' to stop us, do you? He's of a mind with us that this needs doin'."

Suddenly Ridge began to smell a plot. It was possible, he decided, that Wyatt Bass was not merely ignoring this attack, but had actually put some of these men up to it. That would explain how they had identified him so easily despite the fact that he was not wearing his badge.

"You're not goin' through with it," Billy repeated insistently.

One of the men nearby reached out as if to take the gun away from the young deputy and shove him out of the way, but that was a mistake. In a flash Billy put the man to his knees with the barrel of his pistol.

"Now Billy," another man began to reason with him. "You jus' go on off from here like your brother had the good sense to do, an' give us a chance to do what we gotta do to this hombre. There won't be no shame in it."

Angrily Billy Bass grabbed a handful of the man's shirt front and jammed the barrel of his pistol into his mouth until he gagged on the cold steel. "There won't be no shame either," he hissed, "in blowin' your damn brains out the back of your skull if you say one more word. Somebody, untie that man!"

The crowd was stupefied for an instant, and then slowly Ridge began to feel the grips on his arms loosen. When his hands were free, he retrieved his pistol from one of the men nearby and jammed it into the stomach of the first man to set all of this in motion. "This one goes to jail," he told Billy. "An' that one you got there, too, I think . . . an' the one on the ground." He glanced around him briefly and asked, "Any other takers? I seen the jail here an' I know there's room for a passel of you."

But suddenly the jam of men had fallen back to a respectful distance. They were still angry, but they could see that the momentum of their attack was gone. If any of them tried anything, two of their number would die immediately, and even more might fall in the shoot-out that would inevitably ensue.

But then a form pushed his way through the crowd to where Parkman and Billy Bass were still tensely holding their prisoners. The spunky performer, Eddie Ray, seemed undaunted even by the deadly tension that hung in the air around these men. Ray seemed to take control of the situation here almost as quickly and easily as he had inside at the beginning of his show.

"I have to admit," he grinned, "that I can't put on anything to match the show you fellows put on here in the street, but I do have a few more tricks in my bag if anybody's interested in coming back inside to see."

"That seems like one helluva good idea," Billy Bass said, still holding his pistol back into the throat of his prisoner. The man with the pistol in his mouth had no objections to Ray's idea either, though he knew he would not be heading back into the opera house himself just then.

Slowly the crowd began to disperse, moving off after Ray so the entertainment could continue inside. When Ridge and Billy finally felt that they could move from the spot where they had made their stand in reasonable safety, they started across the tracks toward the town marshal's office to lock up their prisoners.

Halfway to the office, one of the three prisoners began mustering his bravado again. He turned his head sideways to mutter, "Your brother'll be fit to be tied when he hears 'bout this, boy, what's with you steppin' in an' screwin' everything up like you done." It was the same man who had pointed out Ridge in the first place, and suddenly Parkman decided he had heard enough from this troublemaker for the night. He holstered his pistol, grabbed the man's arm, and spun him around abruptly. He crashed his right fist into his opponent's belly, and then as the man doubled over in pain, brought his right knee up and smashed him in the face, laying him out cold in the middle of the street.

"Man, that felt good," Ridge grinned over at Billy. "I don't think I coulda slept tonight if I hadn't had the chance to do somethin' like that."

Billy shot a grin back at Parkman, then turned to their other two prisoners and ordered, "You carry him. And if I hear a peep from either of you 'fore we get to the jail, you'll sleep tied to your bunk tonight with a sock stuffed in your mouth. Now get movin'!"

CHAPTER SEVEN

For the next several days, nobody saw much of Marshal Ridge Parkman around Cornersville, Kansas. He stayed out of town a lot, scouting the miles of rolling prairies and farmland to the south and west of town in case a knowledge of that terrain became necessary at some time in the future. He even camped out occasionally at night along the various riverbanks and creek cuts he encountered at sunset.

When he was in town, he stayed in his room much of the time, sometimes even having his meals and an occasional bottle of liquor brought to him so he did not have to walk the streets of town any more than necessary. When he did venture out, it was usually early in the morning, and then only to walk down to Mabel's Café for a hearty, leisurely breakfast. At that hour of the day, most of the people he encountered were the more substantial and settled residents of Cornersville, the folks least likely to give him any trouble or to provoke him to any violent action.

Parkman had two dominant reasons for his new inconspicuous strategy in town, but neither of them had much to do with a fear of being killed by any hothead Texan bent on stopping him from arresting Rakestraw.

One important reason for staying out of sight was a

simple wish not to have to kill anybody or make any more arrests before he had his chance to take Rake-straw into custody. Now, after the incident the night of Eddie Ray's show, word was widespread about who he was and what he had come to do, and the very sight of him would be like the red cape before the bull to the hordes of cowboys who packed the town. In their minds theirs was the just cause, and any man who gunned Parkman down or died trying would be a hero in the eyes of most of his fellow trail hands.

Ridge wanted to try his damnedest not to have to kill any brave but brash young man who pictured himself launching out to fight a just battle in the name of Texas and cowboys everywhere.

Wyatt Bass was the second reason why Parkman stayed out of sight as much as possible. After the night of the show, he was not entirely sure he could control his temper the next time he ran into Bass, and he knew there was no use having to deal with the situation if it could be avoided. The three cowboys he and Billy had arrested were released on a minimal bond the morning after their capture and had quickly left town. But after some deliberation, Ridge had decided to let that slide in the light of his more important mission.

The three, after all, had been no more than the per-sonification of the general attitude toward Parkman, and the mere fact that they had backed down and went to jail was enough to make the point Ridge wanted to make. Looking back on that night, he realized that only the merest thread of good fortune had kept him from dying, and he felt in his own mind that he really had nobody to blame but himself for getting caught up in the midst of such a drunken and emotional crowd of trail hands. If he had died, it would have been due as much to his own carelessness as anything else.

It was hard sometimes to be constantly watchful, to always have to be cautious and on guard even at the most casual moments, always thinking and analyzing, always expecting danger from unexpected sources. But not to live that way often meant not living at all, especially for a man in the violent profession Ridge Parkman had chosen. He had seen it happen to friends and enemies alike. Parkman had made such mistakes before; more times than he could count he had faced death only a hair's breadth away and had sometimes known that his own carelessness was to blame for the situation.

He knew it would probably happen again, too. He was, after all, just a man, as mortal and as capable of error as any other man. But experience did make some difference. Seldom, at least, did he make the same mistake twice.

Ridge sat atop President Grant on a small rise a short distance from Cornersville, gazing northward toward the town. Before him, more than a mile away, a dozen or more cowboys were rousing their herd of hundreds of Texas longhorns from the night bedding ground, lining them out for the short trip on to the holding pens in town. The herd had been stopped on the south bank of the Arkansas River for a couple of days of final grazing and watering and were now ready for the last leg of their journey to the packing houses in northern cities like Kansas City.

The crossing here was a fairly easy one. The river was flat and broad, and the approaches were gradual.

Seldom were any cattle lost during the Arkansas crossing. Beyond lay Cornersville about three miles in the
distance, looking small and insignificant on the broad
expanse of Kansas prairie.

Ridge had been on a two-day scouting trip far down
the cattle trail from Texas, trying to determine if any
of the herds close by were the one he was waiting for.
He had camped the night before along an isolated
creek four or five miles south of where he was at the
moment, and he was headed back into town now for
another day or two of self-imposed isolation. Time was
beginning to weigh heavily on his hands. He had been
in the area ten days now—ten days of troubles and
conflicts—and still he was no closer to accomplishing
his assignment than he had been the first night he rode
into town.

On his third day in town Ridge had switched his
living quarters from the back room in the cantina to
a more secure room in one of the small hotels in a
quieter part of town. With public sentiment so strongly
against him in town, he felt better sleeping in a room
with second-floor windows and a door that locked. As
an added bonus, he enjoyed the luxury of sleeping in
a bed with no lice or stench, and in an area where the
crack of gunfire was not a frequent occurrence all
through the night.

When he got back to town after his two-day explora-
tion, he rode President Grant to the livery stable. After
giving the horse a generous portion of oats and a
thorough rubdown, he started across town toward his
new room. He wasn't particularly looking forward to
remaining in the small room all through the hottest
part of the day, but he kept reminding himself that it
was only for three or four more days. When Rake-

straw's outfit hit town, he was hoping that he could make the arrest quickly and leave town immediately. To try to keep his prisoner in the city jail even for a night would be a very risky proposition at best, even if Wyatt Bass would allow him to lock him up there at all. But Ridge had devised a plan to get Rakestraw out of town quickly, catching a northbound passenger train, then leaving it at some town up the line and starting back south toward Texas on horseback. It would be a perilous journey because Rakestraw's crew would probably dog their trail the whole way, but it was the best idea he could come up with. If he got as far south as Dallas, then perhaps he could call on the marshal's office there for help, or possibly even surrender his prisoner to them and head back north to Denver.

He had stopped for tobacco in a small general store down the street from his hotel and was about to head on down to his room when he spotted the men. There were three of them, lounging around in front of a barbershop which was directly across the street from his hotel.

For a moment he just stood in the doorway of the store and studied them, sensing that this situation might contain danger. There was something unnatural here, something which was not quite as it should be. Then it hit him. It was the wrong part of town to find cowboys loafing, and it was too early in the morning for them to be out and about. He could see the faces of two of the men but did not recognize them. One was a middle-aged man, his face lined and leathery from years of practicing his trade in all sorts of burning heat and brittle cold. He wore his pistol with the holster hanging almost in front of him in the manner of the old-style working cowboys; and though Ridge figured he would not be such a fast man on the draw, he would be a tough opponent on the long haul.

The other was considerably younger, a quick-triggered, swaggering type who probably fancied himself as something of a fast-draw expert. His holster was tied down low on his right leg in the style of a gun-fighter, but Ridge figured that of the two, he would be the easiest to take out in a scrap.

But the third man, who still had his back turned, commanded most of Ridge's attention. It was from him that Ridge most strongly sensed trouble and danger. Then, when he finally turned and glanced down the street in Ridge's direction, the lawman's suspicions were confirmed. It was the man who had pointed Ridge out in the crowd the night of Eddie Ray's show, and the man that he had cold cocked on the way to jail.

The moment their eyes met across the hundred feet which separated them, Ridge knew that their presence was no mere coincidence. They were waiting for him to return to his hotel room.

Ridge dropped his saddlebags beside him and took his Winchester Carbine in both hands, holding it at the ready position. "You lookin' for me?" he called out loudly.

"We damn sure are," the man said, his hand dropping down near his holster as he turned fully around to face Ridge. He started to take a step forward, but Ridge levered a cartridge into the chamber of the Winchester and said, "I can hear you fine from where you're at."

This was a development the three of them had not anticipated. The distance between them would be a very difficult shot for a man with a pistol, but an easy one for Parkman and his Winchester. During their moment's hesitation, Ridge's eyes quickly scanned the rooftops facing him and the alleys nearby, trying to spot any hidden gunman who might have come along with these three as insurance.

Not surprisingly, it was the younger man in the group who first began spouting off with a lot of tough talk, not realizing as the other two did what an advantage their opponent had over them at the moment. Squaring off like a dime-novel badman, he said, "You ain't takin' Jake Rakestraw back to hang. We're here to make sure you don't."

Ridge did not even bother to answer, which seemed to infuriate the brash young man. "What've you got to say to that, mister big-shot lawman?" he taunted.

"Nothin'," Ridge told him. This was a fight. There was no doubt about it, and he did not see any reason to stand here arguing for a while before it started.

The young man began moving sideways out into the street, and even from that distance, Ridge could see his body quivering from the tension of the moment. "I can take you!" he shouted out almost desperately.

"No, Paul!" one of his companions warned him. "Not this way, you little fool!" But it was too late. Paul had already begun his draw.

He was fairly fast, but his accuracy left something to be desired. He got off two shots while Ridge was raising the Winchester to his shoulder, but it was Ridge's bullet that connected. The young man uttered a muted, "Uhhhh," as the bullet struck his body, and it was the last sound he ever made on earth.

But the death of their companion gave the two other men a valuable instant in which to scramble for a better fighting position. As the man Ridge had arrested made a dive for the safety of a nearby horse trough, the older cowboy snapped off a couple of quick shots at Ridge, then broke and ran across the street and ducked into an alley. Ridge snapped off two rounds at the second man, but missed him. Then he dropped to the store's board porch, rolled off the edge of it, and scrambled between the heavy stone pilings under the porch and store.

For an instant nobody moved and the street was deathly quiet. Then the man behind the trough fired a couple of times at Ridge, but he could not see him clearly and the bullets embedded themselves harmlessly in the dirt.

Parkman realized that he would soon be in a very difficult spot here. In a moment his two opponents would have maneuvered themselves until they were on either side of him where they could trap him in a crossfire. The only solution he could see was to take them out one at a time before that could happen.

He snapped off a couple of rounds with the Winchester to keep the man behind the trough down, then rolled sideways under the store until he had reached the edge of the building on one side. There he hunkered down with his back against one of the thick stone pilings, knowing that neither of the other two men would be sure exactly where he was, and there he waited. In a moment he spotted what he had hoped he would see. A pair of legs raced from an adjoining building to the back of the store, then began creeping along cautiously, easing toward the alley on the opposite side.

Parkman brought the rifle to his shoulder, took careful aim, and put a bullet in each leg just below the knee. When the cowboy fell, writhing in pain and grabbing clumsily at his wounds, he spotted Parkman beneath the building.

"You've ruined me, you son of a bitch," the older cowboy rasped out throatily.

Parkman did not answer. He was watching the place where the man's pistol had dropped, hoping he would not go for it. Finally, as the cowboy's fingers began snaking out toward the weapon, Ridge said, "Don't!"

The cowboy paused a moment, cast a hateful glance in Ridge's direction and muttered, "Aw, what the hell."

As he made a grab for the gun, Ridge's rifle exploded again. The cowboy's head snapped sideways from the impact of the bullet and he rolled limply on his back.

As quiet again settled over the area, Ridge wriggled around until he was once more facing the street where the fight had started. He saw no sign of movement from the horse trough where the third man had hid, but he was betting that he was still back there. Ridge judged this character to be no great shucks for bravery, preferring the safety of numbers when there was a dangerous job to be done. The marshal was literally betting his life that the man had chosen to remain where it was safe rather than to move in closer and go for the kill on his own.

Carefully he raised the Winchester, aimed it at the top center of the trough, and waited. Time was on his side now, and both of them knew it. The noise from the gunfight would soon bring at least one of the town's lawmen here to investigate, and when that happened the man behind the trough would be forced either to flee from his hiding place or surrender and go to jail.

Finally the man behind the trough could stand it no longer. "Heck?" he called out. "Did you get 'im, Heck?"

Ridge stayed silent, and in a moment a gun raised up from behind the trough and the man fired blindly in the direction of the store. Ridge held his fire, keeping his aim where it was.

"Holler out, Heck, so's I don't shoot you by mistake," the man called out. An edge of desperation was entering his voice. "Did you get 'im?"

It was an unlucky day for the besieged cowboy, the worst and last he would ever experience. If he had chosen to crawl to one end or the other of the trough and make a break for it, he might have had a faint chance of surviving while Parkman swung his rifle around and fired. But he chose instead to rise to his feet behind the middle of the trough and dash toward a doorway nearby. When he appeared, Parkman's sights were dead center on the middle of his back, and he only gained a couple of steps before the marshal's three bullets marched up his spine.

The fight was over, but for a minute Ridge Parkman did not stir from the spot where he lay. Slowly, expectedly, the trembling began in his arms and shoulders, and soon his hands were shaking so violently that he had trouble holding onto his rifle.

It was a horrible thing to take a life, an awesome sickening tragedy. As he lay there, gazing at the carnage he had created, he felt his stomach churn and tears gathered in his eyes to blur his vision. *Seems like a man'd be used to it by now,* Parkman thought, *especially after being in this business as long as I've been. But I ain't.*

During a fight he was generally all right. Then it

was all method and careful calculation. It was applying all the wits he had, and every ounce of courage he could muster, in order to survive. During a fight he functioned with cold mechanical competence, killing when he had to without compassion or hesitation.

It was always later when the horror of what he had done came crashing in on him. It was a dreadful thing to kill a man.

"Ridge! Are you all right?"

He stirred, and his fingers tightened on the stock of the Winchester. His head raised and his eyes looked up into the concerned face of Billy Bass.

"When I saw you layin' under there with your head down," Billy said with relief, "I thought they'd got you for sure. What happened?"

Glancing around, Ridge saw that people were beginning to filter out of the nearby shops and businesses to stand around and gaze in fascination at the mutilated bodies of the dead men.

"What happened?" Billy asked again.

"They were waitin' for me when I came back from ridin'," Ridge told the deputy, crawling out from under the porch at last and rising to his feet. "The one over there by the trough is one that we locked up the other night. I never seen the other two before."

"Other two?" Billy questioned, glancing at the body of the young man in the street and then beginning to look around the area for the body of the third man.

"He's back there behind the store," Ridge told him.

"Okay, I'll send someone for the coroner," Billy replied, and then added ominously, ". . . and for Wyatt. We'll need to round up some witnesses, I guess, and put together a coroner's hearing."

But Ridge was already a step ahead of him. Spotting the barber across the street gazing at the dead man near the trough, Ridge went over to him. "Come with me," he ordered in a voice that left no room for protest. They marched back across the street to the general store, where Ridge got pencil and paper and asked the barber, "Can you write?"

"Sure, Marshal," the barber told him. "I can write jus' fine."

"Then write down everything you saw just as you saw it," Ridge ordered. Then he turned to the store-keeper and said, "You, too. Everything you can remember an' everything you heard."

Ridge watched over the barber's shoulder for a moment as the man began laboriously printing out his account.

Three men was out front of my shop for about a hour. Then Marshal Parkman come out of the general store. Then one of the men said they'd stop him from hanging Ned Rakestraw. Then one of the men went out in the street . . .

Parkman stayed with the men long enough to assure himself that the two were getting the events down exactly as they had happened. He wanted their accounts recorded while it was all still fresh in their minds, and before anybody else got to them and persuaded them to alter their recollections. Then he went back out in the street to see what Billy Bass was up to.

The young deputy had instructed several bystanders to bring all three bodies together and to lay them side-by-side in the street in front of the barbershop. A crowd of more than twenty people were now standing around, gazing at the corpses.

As Billy surveyed the three riddled bodies, he murmured to Parkman, "Damn, Ridge. You play for keeps, don't you?"

"It makes you sick, don't it?" Ridge mumbled. "You know any of 'em?"

"I jus' know of 'em," Billy said. "The young one there, we run him out of town a couple of months back for carvin' up one of the whores down on the south side."

"He talked big an' shot poor," Ridge said. "His kind never lasts long."

"An' the other one there," Billy went on, indicating the man who had died by the horse trough, "I thought he'd lit out north when Wyatt let him out of jail the other day. He musta sneaked back in."

"It was this other one I hated shootin'," Ridge admitted, pointing to the older man of the three. "Who's he?"

"Name's Heck Zinnaker," Billy replied, and then he added with a significant glance at Ridge. "He's Ned Rakestraw's segundo, second in command of the Circle Bar G outfit. He rode on ahead to line up pasture an' pens for the herd. He just got in this mornin' an' stopped by the office to chat for a while with Wyatt."

"An' he heard about me there, I guess," Ridge said. "That explains why he was waitin' out here with this other trash, layin' for me. I didn't think he fit in with them other two."

"I guess he thought he'd be doin' Rake a favor if he took you out," Billy speculated.

"But instead he died for nothin'," Parkman said. "Too bad."

When the coroner arrived and took charge of the scene, Ridge went back in the store and found his witnesses just finishing their statements. He had the two men sign the bottoms of their pages, then folded both accounts and put them away in his pocket.

Before letting them go, he told them, "Now you've jus' done what's called a 'sworn statement.' No matter how many times you have to tell 'bout this to the coroner or Bass or anybody else official, you tell it jus' the same way you put it down here. If you change your story, that's called perjury an' judges generally don't like it worth a damn."

When he went back outside once more, he saw that Wyatt Bass had reached the scene. The tall city marshal was standing, gazing down at the riddled body of Heck Zinnaker with a massive scowl on his face. When Bass spotted Parkman, he turned to him furiously and demanded, "Just what the hell do you think you're doin' here, Parkman?"

"It's called stayin' alive," Parkman told him, "an it seems to take up a right smart of a man's time here in your town."

"Heck Zinnaker was one helluva good man," Bass said. "There wasn't no finer to be found nowhere around."

"Like Rakestraw?" Parkman asked. "It 'pears to me that all the good men you know got the same bad habit of goin' around slingin' lead at folks. This Zinnaker fellow that you liked so much, he come here to kill me, but I got him first. That's the plain simple facts of the thing and frankly, Bass, I don't give a hoot in hell whether you believe it or not. I got statements here to back up my story."

Billy Bass had been standing nearby, nervously witnessing the confrontation between the two men. Finally he stepped forward and said, "Wyatt, I've been asking some of the folks around and they say Ridge didn't have no choice."

Bass turned his head to give his brother a frown, but they all knew there was no way for him to put any blame for the deaths on Parkman. But that only increased his anger.

Finally, with his fury hanging over them like a lit stick of dynamite, Wyatt Bass said, "Damn you, Parkman! Damn your worthless hide! You just better watch every step you take in my town. Watch every move you make, 'cause you can bet I'll be watchin' too, ready to jump in an' grind your ass into the dust the first time you slip up."

CHAPTER EIGHT

Wyatt Bass kicked Felicia out of bed at three in the morning. He had come in a short time earlier, drunk, tired, a little queasy, and with his knuckles aching from the harsh beating he had given a cowboy that night in the Dixie Darling. Felicia was snoring slightly as he entered, and in Bass's eyes she looked like hell with her face unpainted and her hair in a tangled mess across the pillows of the bed. In the ugly mood he was in, the sight of the girl had been quite repulsive to him, and in a fit of rage he hauled the startled young woman up from the mattress, cursed her for her unconscious transgressions, slapped her a couple of times in punishment, and shoved her out the door of his bedroom.

But as soon as he had undressed and piled into the bed alone, he immediately began to miss her presence there beside him. A couple of times he bellowed out her name, hoping that she was still waiting outside the door, but she was either too frightened to come back or had gone off in search of some other room in which to spend the night. His roaring commands went unanswered.

With the room swirling about him, Bass had finally drifted toward sleep, cursing Ridge Parkman heatedly in his thoughts. In his mind Parkman was to blame even for this. If Parkman had not come to town, if he had not remained so insistent about the Rakestraw thing, defying, intimidating, or gunning down all opposition, then all these lousy things would not be happening to Bass. If not for Parkman's presence, Bass would not have gotten drunk tonight, would not have so badly mutilated that hapless cowboy, and would not have abused and rejected his soft, warm bedmate. Parkman was to blame for him having to sleep alone tonight, and Bass vowed to himself that very soon all this chaos and disruption would come to an end one way or another.

The next morning was not much better. Paul Halliday appeared at his bedside entirely too early, scarcely atoning for his sin by bringing a pot of coffee and two mugs with him. Halliday at least had the good sense to stay quiet while his partner choked down the first cup and knocked the edge off his stupor, but Bass was still scarcely able to focus his thoughts clearly when the gambler started in on him.

"Wyatt, you're walkin' a thin plank over a deep gulley," Halliday reprimanded him sternly.

"Shut up, Paul," Bass snarled at him, but the order lacked conviction, and Halliday was not about to comply until he had his say.

"That was a damned stupid thing you did last night, gettin' so drunk. The doc was still at work this morning tryin' to piece that cowboy back together, an' his friends are mad as hornets about it. Billy had all he could handle to keep them from comin' after you, an' he ended up spendin' the night downstairs with a shotgun just to make sure. How does it feel havin' your baby brother play nursemaid to you 'cause you got yourself so likkered up you couldn't take care of yourself anymore?"

"Nobody asked him to," Bass stormed out angrily. "I can take care of myself just fine. Always could an' always will."

For a moment Halliday just sat in his chair near the bed, staring at Bass with a critical, skeptical look in his eye. Finally Bass swung his legs off the side of the bed, drew a deep breath as if facing some difficult task, and rose to his feet. It had been some time since Halliday had seen his friend undressed, and he was surprised to discover how much Bass had gone to paunch and sag. The time had been when Bass was all lean, firm muscle, as hard as a steam locomotive and nearly as powerful. But the good life here had been a little too good, and it was beginning to show on the marshal's thirty-five-year-old body.

"That damn Parkman," Bass muttered as he fumbled around the room in search of his clothes. He probed in his closet for a moment, then asked, "Where in the hell's my white suit? I told that little whore to have it ready for me to wear today, but she can't do anything right."

Halliday watched with concern for a moment longer, feeling an odd anxiety flowing through him unexpectedly. Finally, he said, "Can't you see it, Wyatt? Can't you see how things have been slidin' downhill lately?"

Bass turned and gave Halliday a dark, critical look and said, "It's just that lousy federal man. He's got everything all screwed up around here. The sooner we get him outa here, the better."

"He's part of it," Halliday agreed, "but he ain't the whole problem. Times are changin' Wyatt, an' we're both gettin' older. Things aren't the way they used to be back in Salinas, an' it's a fact we both better start gettin' used to."

Bass pulled a dark brown suit out of the closet and laid it on the bed, then turned to Halliday. "You're talkin' like a scared ol' woman, Paul," he accused. "So he got lucky an' killed three men without gettin' a scratch on him. So what? That don't mean he can't die just like any other man. You an' I both know I've faced up to men a lot tougher than this son of a bitch an' took 'em out with no sweat."

As he talked, his voice grew louder and his tone became more intense, as if he was trying to convince not only Halliday of his skill and invincibility but also himself.

"Have you forgotten how it was when we first come here, the way I cleaned up this town all by myself? I killed four men in the first week, nine in the first month. I hit this town kickin' ass an' layin' down rules, an' when I got done I had it right here." He turned the thumb of his right hand down as if using it to squash a bug. "But if I want to get drunk once in a while an' blow off a little extra steam, I've got a right, too. A man needs that sometimes when things start pilin' up on him."

"You didn't used to need it, Wyatt," Halliday told him quietly.

"To hell with 'used to'," Bass stormed. "Things have changed."

"That's what I've been tryin' to tell you. But they haven't changed the way you think."

"Paul, why don't you just get the hell outa here an' leave me alone? I really don't need to hear all this panty-waist moanin' an' complainin' right now. Not this early in the mornin'. Go downstairs an' count money or go get a drink or get laid or somethin'. Just leave me alone!"

"Not yet," Halliday exclaimed. "Not 'til I say what I came here to say." He paused and waited until he was sure he had Bass's complete attention. Then he proclaimed solemnly, "I'm gonna kill Parkman. My mind's made up."

For a moment Bass did not answer as he finished dressing and went to a mirror hanging on the wall to run a comb through his thick black hair. When that was done, he took his holster and the legendary pair of pearl-handled revolvers down from a hook by the door and strapped them on. When he turned back to his friend at last, the metamorphosis was complete. He was again Wyatt Emerson Bass, the awesome city marshal of Cornersville, Kansas, tamer of half a dozen rambunctious Kansas towns.

"Since when do you tell me what you're goin' to do?" he asked Halliday quietly and threateningly. The fury was gone now, and the aura of invincibility seemed to have returned. But still Halliday had his doubts. He couldn't put the picture of Bass's ponderous gut, sagging down over the tops of his underwear, out of his mind. *It had been too good here for too long.*

"He's gotta die, Wyatt, an' you're not the one to do it. It'd spoil everything here if you were the one that took him out."

"No man ever had to fight my fights for me. Not ever."

"But it's not just your fight. It's mine, too, an' everybody that has to go on livin' in this town after he's gone.

"I've got it all worked out in my head how it'll go. Rakestraw's only two or three days out of town, an' if

Parkman dies now, the marshals won't have time to send another lawman here before the Circle Bar G herd is sold an' Ned Rakestraw is on his way back home. After that he's on his own. An' if I take Parkman out quiet like in the middle of the night, then you can wire the news out to Kansas City an' make a big show of lookin' for his killer. You'll be in the clear all the way."

"You know what you're sayin', Paul?" Bass asked seriously. "I'm a lawman, an' you're talkin' to me about murderin' a lawman in cold blood."

"The man's a killer," Halliday rationalized. "Hell, I think he's about half crazy. Lawmen can go sour, too, an' when they do, they gotta be took out just like any other bad hombre that's too dangerous to leave alive. It's what's good for Cornersville, an' it's what's good for you an me, too."

Bass just stood staring at his friend intently for a moment. The whole idea of what Halliday was suggesting was repulsive to him, but he could find no error in the logic of his reasoning. Parkman was definitely a dangerous man, a destructive force who threatened the peace and stability of this entire town. Maybe he should die this way. At last Bass turned and started for the door. He gripped the handle, but before going out, he turned to Halliday and said, "I don't want to know when or who or where. I don't want to know anything about it."

The world really was not such a bad place. Not all of it. There were a lot of good folks around, the ones who tried to live right and never hurt anybody unless there was a good reason to do it. It was that kind of people that Ridge Parkman considered himself working for, and whenever he sorely needed a friend, it always seemed like there was some decent soul around to offer the hand of friendship.

Mabel Cain was such a person. He had sensed it from the first, but now as his situation became more tense and the critical time of Rakestraw's arrival grew closer, he found himself increasingly relying on Mabel as one of the few bright spots in an otherwise bleak and desperate atmosphere. Parkman considered himself pretty much a loner, but he knew that even loners needed to be around others once in a while. There wasn't a person alive who didn't occasionally crave the sound of another human voice and the sight of a friendly smile.

But Parkman put severe limitations on the amount of time he spent with Mabel, partly so he would not make a nuisance of himself and partly because he did not want to bring the danger that seemed to dog him constantly any closer to her than necessary. He saw her just about every morning when he went down to her place for breakfast, and he also went down occasionally at closing time to walk her home and then sit around her small house drinking coffee and talking.

Mabel seemed to realize and appreciate the fact that she was a curiously necessary part of Ridge Parkman's life at this very unstable time. Unlike many of her fellow business owners in Cornersville, she refused to shun him, and he had the peculiarly gratifying sensation that she would be willing to defy the great Wyatt Emerson Bass and this whole town in order to befriend a person she liked.

Now on the evening of the second day after the shoot-out in front of the hotel, Ridge had again found his way to Mabel's Café at closing time. Since killing the three men he had gone through a day-long bout of depression alone in his room, and he thought it was about time to stir out into the town once more to seek the pleasant company of his female friend.

On his way there, he had stopped in a small saloon to pick up a pint of the best whiskey the place had to offer, and he now had that hidden away in his shirt pocket under his jacket. On his second visit to Mabel's home, she had revealed one of her most closely guarded secrets. When she drank her customary last cup of coffee in the evening, there wasn't always just coffee in the cup. Mabel liked her toddies, but she would have been mortified if the people in the town had discovered she was a "tippler," as she called it, and she often did without the little jolt of liquor she enjoyed simply because there was no discreet way for her to get her hands on it. After that, Ridge always carried a full bottle with him, and left the unused portion behind when he went away.

When he entered the restaurant and slouched down into a chair near the door to wait for closing, he saw that there was only one customer still there, a dusty-bedraggled cowboy who had apparently just reached town and was enjoying a late supper before beginning to explore the local night life.

Ridge was glad when the man glanced back at him without any spark of recognition in his eyes. The cold hostility of this town, the ugly looks, the muttered curses, and veiled threats were beginning to drain away his patience, and he could feel a dangerously explosive anger beginning to accumulate deep within him. Three men had already died, but that total could rise if anybody in this town did just the wrong thing to set him off. He had taken just about all he could take without beginning to strike back.

But Mabel's warm smile made him feel better. She was in the back wiping down the checkered tablecloths and finishing the last of her clean-up chores before closing. As Ridge waited, the spry, elderly black woman who helped Mabel with the cooking came out of the kitchen and bid Ridge goodnight before going out the front door on her way home.

At last the cowboy mopped the last of the gravy from his plate with a biscuit, slugged back the remaining coffee in his mug, and rose to leave. After Mabel cleared his dishes from the table, she came back to Ridge and said, "I guess that's it. Do you feel like stopping by the place for a cup tonight?"

"I was hopin' you'd ask," he told her with a grin. "Seems like I been hangin' 'round you a good bit lately but danged if it isn't good to spend a few minutes a day 'round somebody I'm sure ain't goin' to haul out some iron an' commence blastin' away."

"Well, you know you're always welcome to come around, Ridge," Mabel said. "Shoot, I hadn't had this much attention from any menfolk since my days up in Golden City when an old prospector died an' word got out in town he'd left me money."

Ridge helped her extinguish the lamps, then they went out and Mabel locked the front door. The route they took to her home led across several dimly lit back streets, and away from the part of town that was the most rowdy and explosive at this time of night. Even where they were, several blocks away from the south side of town, they could hear the loud music, roaring crowds and occasional shots from the saloon district where things were just beginning to peak for the night.

"Everybody in the place was talking about your shoot-out today," Mabel told Ridge. "From the versions that was told to me, you're either one of the most lowdown backshooters that ever had the gall to show his face around decent folks, or the most golddarned hand with firearms that ever pinned on a badge."

"I bet the opinion in this town generally tends to lean toward the first description," Ridge said.

"Yeh, I'm afraid that's so," Mabel said. "But every chance I got, I put folks straight about what kind of fellow you are."

"Wal, thanks, Mabel," he said. "But don't get yourself in no hot water over me. Don't forget, I'll jus' be doin' my job an' movin' on, but you got to stay here an' live 'round these folks."

"Dang it, I don't care, Ridge. It seems to me that your coming here has pointed out a lot of things to us local folks, if we just got enough sense to open up our eyes and see them. There's so many folks in this town dead set on stopping a good man from doing what's right, that it seems like there's just gotta be something bad wrong with the way this whole place is set up. I don't even know if I'll be stayin' after."

That pronouncement startled Ridge. When he started out for Cornersville, he had no idea that his simple task of arresting a cowboy could bring about such upheaval in a whole community, but at times it seemed as if his mission had become the focal point of the entire area's existence. Now even Mabel was talking about leaving after he got ahold of Rakestraw. The whole thing was befuddling.

"It bothers me to hear you say somethin' like that," Ridge admitted to her. "I never set out to change nobody's life by what I gotta do here, 'cept maybe Ned Rakestraw's life. It didn't ever cross my mind that this kind of mess could be stirred up jus' 'cause a man had to be took in to face trial for a murder. Look what's happened already. Three men are dead that didn't really have to be, an' there's no guarantee that it'll stop there. I feel like I jus' dropped a match by accident and lit some kind of hellacious prairie fire that still don't show no signs of burnin' itself out. But I don't know what to do 'bout it."

"The answer is you don't do anything except the job you came here to do," Mabel said. "You didn't make the mess here. You just stepped into the middle of it and showed us that it was a mess. We've been depending on the Texas cattle for our income for a dozen years or more, but it seems like now it's just taken over our lives. The people who live in Cornersville don't own their town anymore, not if they sit back and let something like this happen. If the day comes when we're afraid for a lawman to come into our town and arrest a murderer, then it seems like everything we've got here has gone bad sour. Maybe it's time for the town to die, or at least for the big money that runs through here to stop flowing. If it took being poor again for us to get back some of the self-respect we used to have, then to my thinking it wouldn't be too big a price to pay."

"Wal, has it ever occurred to anybody that maybe this whole town is runnin' scared for no good cause?" Ridge asked. "Maybe when I get Rakestraw an' haul him off, everything will jus' go back to the way it was before."

"Maybe for a while it will," Mabel said. "But what everybody in town is trying to ignore is the fact that time's working against us. With the whole country growing and building all over the place, and with the railroads scattering out new tracks every whichaway, our days as a rail's-end boomtown have to be numbered. But when it starts, you can bet this time will be remembered, and in the minds of some, you'll always be the boogeyman that brought Cornersville to her knees." She paused and looked at Ridge with a gaze that was more intense and tender than any other she had ever given him. "That is," she added, "if you get done what you set out to do."

"It's a big if," Ridge admitted.

They had passed out of the main business section of the north side of town and started down an alley which was a shortcut to the street that Mabel lived on. The alley was nearly pitch-black, and here, only two blocks from her house, the noise from the south side of town had grown more distant.

There were certain instincts that most men who lived with guns as tools of their trade or as a means of survival firmly believed in. Shooting was one such instinct. The best shots seldom raised their weapon and sighted along the barrel before firing. They just pointed and let go, knowing that the instincts they had developed over the years would take care of the direction that the bullet went. The best could put all six shots from their revolver into an area the size of a playing card at fifty feet or more and never raise their weapon above waist height.

And there were other instincts that made the difference between who lived and died in this violent western land. Parkman had once heard an old trapper swear that the legendary Jim Bridger could sense the presence of an Indian farther than most men could see one. And Parkman could easily believe such a thing. Bridger had put in fifty years as a trapper, trader, Indian fighter, scout, and mountain man, and had survived to go back to Missouri and live out his old age spinning yarns from a rocking chair.

Ridge Parkman was a firm believer in instincts, and in following up on the momentary premonitions that occasionally came suddenly to him. Too many times just that instant of instinctive warning had spelled the difference between life and death to him.

And now such a warning was coming to him in the midst of the dark alley. He felt it as surely as if a hand had reached out from nowhere and slapped him. It could have been a sound so faint or a movement so subtle that it only registered in his subconscious, or it could have been merely the warning of experience that such places sometimes contained danger. But whatever it was, only two or three steps into the alley, Parkman paused and tensed, reaching out for Mabel's arm so she would go no farther.

"What's the matter?" she asked, sensing his sudden shift in mood.

"I don't know," he answered, his eyes seeking to drill a hole in the blackness ahead of them. He stood dead still for a moment, then finally told her urgently, "Get back to the street an' find some safe place to hide!"

But Mabel did not have time to comply with the order. The streak of light, the roar of the pistol, and the searing slice of pain along the ribs of Ridge's left side all happened at the same instant. Ridge swung his right arm around violently, striking Mabel across her chest and knocking her flat on her back, then dived forward and drew his revolver. More shots roared out, but where a moment before both he and Mabel had been outlined against the lighter shade of the buildings behind them, now there was no clear target for the hidden gunman to aim at. His shots only served to pinpoint his location in the darkness.

Parkman heard a scuffling behind him and knew that it was Mabel crawling away to safety. In a moment she whispered to him, "I'm safe now, Ridge. Go ahead and get him."

That was the news he had been waiting to hear. Slowly, not making any noise that could be heard above the distant commotion coming from the south side of town, he began crawling forward on his stomach, staying close to the wall of a building on one side. The shots had come from about twenty-five feet away and low on the opposite side, but from the faint scuffling noises that Ridge heard ahead, he guessed that the gunman had changed his position after the last series of shots.

But he sensed that the gunman was not ready to abandon the fight and flee just because the first shots had not reached their target, and if that was so, then Parkman knew he was facing a determined, confident opponent. Cautiously he continued to inch forward, taking his time and making no sound that would reveal his location. A moment before the darkness had given the hidden attacker all the advantage, but now that neither of them was sure exactly where the other was that advantage was gone.

The silent forward progress was slow, but it was the only way. Firing blindly in the darkness would be a foolish move, and Parkman much preferred to wait patiently for the other man to make some minute sound that would reveal his location. He got to within what

he guessed must be about ten feet from the place
where the first shots were fired, then stopped and lay
still on the ground, his Peacemaker cocked and waiting.

The moments dragged by. It was possible, Parkman knew, that the other man had somehow slipped
out of the alley and fled, but he was not going to take
any chances. If it took waiting here until dawn just
to make sure, then he was prepared to do just that.

And then a remarkable thing happened suddenly
and unexpectedly. In the middle of the street beyond
the other end of the alley, a crash sounded out and
a ball of flame leaped into the air higher than a man's
head. In the eerie light of that explosion he spotted
his opponent immediately, crouched down behind a
stack of crates with only part of his head and his revolver protruding out. With the fire behind him and
the deadly U.S. marshal in front, the moment of confusion and indecision that the man experienced spelled
his ruin.

Parkman fired one shot at the protruding head, then
swung his revolver slightly and pumped two more
shots into the crates where the man's body had to be.
Then he rolled one quick turn to the side, aimed his
pistol again, and snapped off a fourth shot as his
opponent rose shakily to his feet and stumbled backward.

With the light now, and his attacker clearly in view,
Parkman finally rose to his feet. His pistol was still
pointed at the downed man, and he was prepared to
fire again at the slightest threatening movement as he
walked forward cautiously and looked at his attacker.

"Ridge?" Mabel called out. Her voice came from

the opposite end of the alley now, but she was still not in sight.

"I got him," Ridge called out. She stepped forward then and started toward him just as he reached in his pocket for a match. In the flickering light it provided Parkman could see that the other man was still alive, though the side of his head and his entire chest were both a bloody mess from the marshal's shots.

"It's Paul Halliday!" Mabel gasped in amazement. "Wyatt's partner." The wounded man was gazing up at them with such a glazed stare that it was difficult to know whether or not he was seeing anything. His punctured chest rose and fell with a sickening, gurgling irregularity.

But Mabel's identification of the attacker had been unnecessary. With teeth-gritting fury, Parkman remembered seeing this smug, dandified character in Bass's office in the saloon the day he had gone to issue his warning to the city marshal. And as Halliday's right arm began to rise weakly up off the ground, Parkman also remembered his suspicions that day that Halliday might have some sort of weapon up the sleeve of his jacket. He stepped forward and pinned the gambler's hand to the ground with his right foot. As they stood there watching for a moment longer, the man's head rolled to the side, his breathing stopped, and he was dead.

"Thanks for the help, Mabel," Parkman said. "The fire was a real smart idea. Neither one of us expected it, but it made all the difference."

"I found an old lamp hanging on a storefront," Mabel told him. "I lit it and carried it around, and then I just pitched it in the middle of the street. So what do we do now?"

"The first thing is," Ridge said, "I'm gettin' you to your house. Don't nobody ever have to know that you had a part in this. It might go hard on you if folks knew."

"I don't care," Mabel pronounced defiantly. "I don't give a hoot in hell if the whole damn town knows I had a part in the killing of this rotten bushwacker."

"We'll do it my way," Ridge said. "From here on out, I'll have all I can do to watch my own backside without havin' to worry 'bout whether some owlhoot might be comin' after you, too."

"Okay, Ridge," Mabel conceded. "Your way, then." Leaving Halliday where he had fallen and died, they left the alley and started hurriedly down the street toward Mabel's house. He needed to get some bandages over the bullet crease on his side, and then he had a visit to make.

The Dixie Darling was unusually quiet tonight. Bass suspected it was because word had gone out about the beating he had given the young cowboy the night before. He was not particularly proud of his actions of the previous night, but he was not about to show that by apologizing to anybody, and he told himself that it would all blow over and things would be back to normal soon.

Felicia was still pouting, too. He had not seen her all day, but he knew she would be back eventually when her pique at him disappeared. She had a good deal going, and Bass knew she was spoiled to the luxurious life-style he provided for her. She was not about to give all that up and go back on the line with the other girls if she could avoid it.

But Paul was the one that worried him the most.

He had never seen Halliday act quite like he had that morning—grave, worried, and almost desperate about something. The change had come quite suddenly, and it seemed now as if his partner thought they were both on the brink of losing everything they had. He had not showed up this evening either, and though that was not uncommon, Bass still wondered in the back of his mind if his friend intended to follow through on what he had vowed earlier. It would be a serious undertaking, and one that the marshal was not too happy about his friend attempting.

It was ten thirty now, the time of night when things should really be underway in the Dixie Darling, but no more than fifteen or twenty customers were scattered about the place, and most of them seemed quiet and sullen tonight. Earlier Bass had struck up a small-stakes card game at one of the back tables, but the meager winnings he had accumulated had brought him no pleasure, and within an hour he had drifted away to sit by himself, somberly nursing a glass of whiskey as he sat glaring out over the room.

He was still missing Felicia, and he began thinking about having one of the other girls go find her, so they could retire to his rooms early and spend the rest of the evening making up at their leisure. It was a pretty sure bet that things were not going to liven up in the saloon for the rest of the night, and he did not believe his services as a peacemaker would be needed. If trouble did come up, he would only be a loud shout away in his quarters upstairs, and Billy was still on duty just a couple of blocks down the street.

Bass scarcely paid any attention when the dust-covered cowboy strode in the door, but when the man glanced around to locate him and then started directly toward his table, the marshal sat up in his chair and casually brushed his right coattail back to expose the handle of his revolver. It was Parkman, and he had a hard, mean look in his eyes. In his left hand he carried a revolver by the barrel, and in his right was a bundle wrapped in a bloodied swatch of cloth.

When Parkman reached the city marshal's table, he threw the revolver down with such force that it bounced off the table and went rattling away on the floor. Then he pitched the bundle down and it fell open, revealing a smaller revolver, a derringer, a flip-blade knife, and a bulging, bloody wallet with a neat bullet hole through the center of it. Bass recognized every item.

"The rest of him's on its way to the undertaker's," Parkman said. His voice had all the warmth and friendliness of a handful of coffin nails rattling down a tin roof.

"Paul Halliday? Dead?" Bass asked in disbelief. The shock of it was overwhelming. He leaned forward as if to rise to his feet, but suddenly Parkman backhanded him across the side of his face with incredible force. As Bass toppled sideways out of his chair, Parkman flung the table aside violently with one hand as his Colt leaped into the other. Before the city marshal could recover from the stunning blow, his antagonist was kneeling beside him, the cold steel of the revolver pressing painfully against the tip of his nose.

By then the entire saloon was watching them in awed silence, but none stepped forward to help Bass out of this incredible predicament.

Parkman's voice was brittle with revulsion and hatred when he spoke again. "I seen some low-down, belly-crawlin', yella skunks in my day," he said, "an some of them had badges pinned on their shirt jus' like I did. But, Bass, you gotta be the slimiest piece of worthless scum that ever had the nerve to call himself a lawman. Four men are dead 'cause you turned out to be such a gutless bastard, an' two of them were close friends of yours. Please . . . *please* . . . do somethin' stupid so I'll have a reason to squeeze this trigger an' blow your stinkin' brains slap out the back of your head!"

Every sound and movement had ceased in the Dixie Darling Saloon. Those who watched Parkman's sudden assault on Bass were now frozen like statues, and in each of their minds was the question of whether in another instant they would witness the unthinkable, the execution of Wyatt Emerson Bass. A minute before it would have been inconceivable that anybody would have had the audacity to come in here and strike their legendary town marshal, let alone draw a gun and threaten him; but now, suddenly, Bass had been struck down and lay defenselessly on the floor, awaiting his fate. Even Matt Rikard, who stood behind the bar with a double-barreled shotgun within easy reach, stood motionless and awestruck.

Then the sound of Bass's voice brought an air of reality back to the scene. "Do it, Parkman," he said. His voice contained no hint of the fear that any ordinary man would have to feel at such a moment. He spoke with the same calm, commanding tone which all were accustomed to hearing from him in dangerous situations. "If you don't kill me now, I'll dog you to the edge of the world 'til I get even with you for this night."

Inches from his face, Bass watched as Parkman's finger tightened an almost imperceptible amount on the trigger of his Colt. He shifted his gaze up until he was staring directly into Parkman's eyes and rarely had he ever seen such an expression of cold violence on anyone's face. This man had been pushed absolutely as far as he could be pushed.

Nobody had noticed Billy Bass step through the swinging front doors of the Dixie Darling, but when he spoke, his voice sliced through the tension in the room like a red-hot blade.

"Don't, Ridge," he said. "If you kill him, you'll die one second later."

"Who cares?" Parkman snarled, never moving. Bass could see him waging a mental war against the almost overwhelming urge to fire the gun.

"That would be how many dead then?" Billy asked. "Five or six? And Ned Rakestraw would still be a free man."

A long tense moment dragged by, but at last Parkman began to rise slowly to his feet. As he started walking backward toward the door, directly at the drawn gun of Billy Bass, he began to sweep the room with his pistol, his eyes connecting to those of every other man there and seeming to ask, "Will you try me? Or you? Or you?"

When he neared the door, Billy stepped back out of the way and Parkman backed on out, never even glancing at the deputy who had covered him the whole time.

After he was gone, Billy stood staring at his brother for a long time, watching as Wyatt got up and dusted off his clothes, asking questions with his eyes which Bass knew he would never be able to answer if they had been put into words.

CHAPTER NINE

The early risers in town spotted him first no more than an hour past dawn. He sat straight and still on his horse atop a small rise about a half mile east of town, vividly silhouetted against the bright illumination of the eastern sky and the rising sun. Everybody knew who it was without having to be told.

He was still there at ten o'clock when Wyatt Bass woke up. The city marshal roused slightly and reached out for Felicia, but found her gone from the bed. When he looked around he saw the young woman standing at the window of their room, which faced east, gazing out in rapt fascination.

"What you lookin' at there, girl?" the marshal asked, still half asleep. "C'mon. Get back in bed."

"He's just sitting there," the girl said quietly. "I've been watching him for half an hour or better, and he's never moved a muscle."

"What in the hell you talkin' about?" Bass asked irritably. Something about the odd tone in her voice made him get up and move over to the window.

"It's like he was on guard or something," Felicia said reverently. "Or like he was watching every move everybody made here in town. It's creepy."

"That's Parkman," Bass announced with disgust. "I

don't know what kinda crap he thinks he's pulling, but at least as long as he stays up there, he's outa town an' outa my hair."

But despite his offhanded comment, what the girl had said was true. It seemed almost as if the distant lawman's attention was focused precisely on this room, watching their movements and hearing their every word. Felicia turned and started to remove her nightgown, then paused, went to the window, and closed the curtains before continuing to undress. Both of them dressed quickly and quietly, feeling the uneasiness which seemed to hang heavily over the entire town.

When Bass got downstairs to his office, he found Mayor Mike Tackett waiting impatiently there for him. As the Mexican maid brought in a pot of coffee and poured cups for the two men, Tackett asked, "Have you seen him, Wyatt?"

"Yeah, I saw him up there. So what?"

"Well, what are you going to do about it? That's what a lot of us want to know right now."

"Nothin'," Bass told him irritably. "That's what I plan to do right now. Exactly nothin'!"

The banker hesitated a moment, taking a swig of his coffee as he studied the marshal curiously over the rim of his upturned cup. What he had to say was not going to be easy, but he had promised the aldermen and some of the businessmen in town that he would have a talk with Bass and try to present their concerns to him. A month ago, such a thing would have been unthinkable to Tackett, but a month ago, Marshal Ridge Parkman had not been here, bringing with him all the uncertainty and dangers which his mission implied.

"There's those around," Tackett said at last, "who're starting to wonder, Wyatt. And they're starting to talk."

"Yeah, Mike? An' what're they sayin'?" Bass asked defiantly.

"They're saying how, slow but sure, things seem to be getting out of control here in Cornersville," the mayor told him. "What with those three killings the other day, and then Paul Halliday last night . . . Hell, Wyatt, we know you couldn't have been there to stop any of them, but both times folks kept looking for you to do something afterward. And what did you do? You sat back and let him knock you on your ass and point a gun in your face."

Bass's venomous glare shot across the room at Tackett like a blazing spear, but it only made the mayor hesitate. It did not shut him up, a fact which was significant to both of them in different ways.

"People are beginning to wonder if you've still got what it takes to keep a lid on trouble here in Cornersville, Marshal. We . . . they're beginning to wonder if you're still the same man we hired to come in here and clean our town up a few years ago."

Bass's face was slowly transforming into a cold mask of hatred and disdain. "I'll tell you what you should do," he said at last, his voice sharp like the bare edge of a blade. "You find somebody else that you think can do a better job, an' you tell him to come here an' take this badge off my chest. If he can handle that, then he can keep the badge an' everything that goes along with it, includin' the job an' this whole town fulla candy-assed cowards."

"Now, Wyatt," the mayor began, wondering if he might have carried his criticism too far. "Nobody's suggesting that we find a replacement for you. We're not forgetting what a good job you've done in the past. It's just that . . ."

"Shut up, Mike," Bass interrupted. "You've run your mouth too much already, an' I'm sick of hearin' it. If I have to sit here an' put up with much more of this, I might start feelin' the strong urge to give you a quick kick out the front door of my place."

"Throwing me out's not going to solve anything, Wyatt," the mayor reasoned. "Nobody doubts that you're tough enough to beat me up and throw me out of anyplace you take a notion to. But the question is, can you handle this Parkman fella as easily? Or can you handle him at all?"

"I'll give you two choices," Bass pronounced at last, impulsively pulling his shiny badge off his jacket and tossing it on the table between them. "You pick that up, or you tell me to put it back on. But if it goes back on my chest, then you understand that I'll handle this business in my own time in my own way. With no interference. What'll it be, Mike?"

The banker studied the badge seriously for a moment, then glanced up at Bass with resignation in his eyes. "Put it back on, Wyatt," he said.

"Please."

"Please, Marshal Bass, pin your badge back on," Tackett said. "But for God's sake, Wyatt . . ."

"My own time. My own way."

Some time past noon, after many of the cowboys had already begun their daily drinking, a group of them gathered along the tracks at the eastern edge of town to gaze toward the distant figure, speculating about what he was up to and discussing among themselves what dire fates he should be subjected to. When one of the men came up with a Winchester and popped off a casual shot toward Parkman, several others thought it was a good idea and hurried away to get their firearms.

Within a few minutes a dozen or more men were lined up, blasting away with a barrage that none of them had any real hopes would reach its target.

But their firing did inspire some motion from Parkman. He had not seemed to move all morning, but now they could tell that he dismounted from his horse and was doing something as he stood beside it. An instant later a bullet struck a rail of the tracks nearby with a startling metallic twang and went singing away. The pop of the marshal's rifle reached them only a fraction of a second later.

Then one of the men grabbed his left side and spun away, and the sound of that shot reached the group before the man had fallen to the ground.

"Hot damn, that's a Sharps 50 he's firing!" one of the men called out, suddenly remembering having seen the long-barreled buffalo gun in a second boot on Parkman's saddle.

"You're right. I remember seein' it," a second man confirmed.

The crowd began hurriedly scattering for cover as a third and fourth shot slammed harmlessly into the dirt in their midst, and the pot-shooting at the far-off man ceased to provide any entertainment for anybody in Cornersville.

Parkman remained there until after sunset, and that night there was some talk in the saloons around town of getting up a group to go out and find his camp. But there was an odd, subdued feeling in town that night, as if the federal marshal had become sort of a phantom who might be found anyplace, or no place at all. Men walking home after dark jumped at shadows in alleys and fired their pistols frantically at unexplained stray noises.

Nobody was anxious to roam out into the hills on this moonless night and back up all the tense, tough talk which was floating around with any action.

At dark, Parkman rode President Grant to the northwest until he reached a small sheltered draw within a few hundred yards of town. With the horse tethered there where it could graze until he returned, he went on foot to the edge of town.

When he reached Mabel Cain's house, he crept in the back door, ate the plate of cold meat and vegetables she had left for him, and went into the front room to grab a few hours of sleep before dawn.

Ty Kitchens didn't like this job worth a damn. He was convinced that because he was the youngest and the most inexperienced man in the trail crew, Ned Rakestraw always gave him the shit work that nobody else wanted to be bothered with. Most of the way up here he had ridden drag, eating the thick clouds of dust from the cattle mile after mile, day after day, until everything he ate and drank had the faint taste of Texas soil to it. Then when the day was ended, he was usually the one assigned to gather wood and chips for the cook, or to tend to the horses of the other men while they marched off to the chuck wagon for coffee and beans.

And now he had been picked again, this time for a job which nearly convinced him that Rakestraw was determined to get rid of him one way or the other.

For better than a week now, all they had been hearing from the groups of cowboys on their way back to Texas was how the U.S. marshal was waiting in Cornersville to arrest their trail boss. Rakestraw had not paid much mind to it, because he had a dozen hard men with him and they were headed into a town that was ruled by one of his closest compadres on God's green earth—Wyatt Bass.

But in the past couple of days the stories had begun to take on a different tone. Some of the cowboys headed in the opposite direction were talking about all the killing this marshal was doing, and Rakestraw really started getting serious when he learned that his own *segundo*, Heck Zinnaker, had been killed in a gunfight with this Parkman fellow. Nobody had even considered asking Rakestraw whether he might turn the herd over to the crew and let them take it in without him. All knew that a couple of dozen devils from hell would have a tough fight in stopping Ned Rakestraw from completing his task of getting the Circle Bar G herd into the Cornersville cattle pens. The talk around the campfires at night was noticeably more somber, and now that Cornersville was near, each man in the outfit was spending a little time each night making sure his firearms were clean, oiled, and in good working condition.

Then the night before, Rakestraw had come over to Ty Kitchens just as he was bedding down for the night and informed him that he would be going on ahead of the herd to carry a message to this marshal in Cornersville. Kitchens listened to his instructions without comment, and he knew better than to protest or question the boss's instructions, but he did his best to let his opinion be known by the hard looks he returned to Rakestraw.

Kitchens was to leave early the next morning and ride straight to Cornersville. Near town, Rakestraw said, he was to unload all his firearms and stow them away so there would be no suspicions that he might be another assassin sent in to take a crack at the marshal.

The message he was to deliver was simple: Rakestraw wanted no trouble, but he was coming in town with his herd and he did not intend to be arrested while he was there.

Now, as Kitchens rode into the edge of the town, he wondered again whether he would live to see another day. He had been tempted not to stop and unload his guns as instructed, thinking that it would be better to die fighting. But at last he decided to do as he had been told. Unless this marshal was a complete maniac, surely he would not gun down an unarmed man.

His first stop was at the city marshal's office. He hoped to find Wyatt Bass there and to perhaps get his advice on the best way to approach Parkman. But when he saw the young man seated behind the desk, he knew immediately that he was too young to be the famous lawman.

"Is Marshal Bass somewhere around?" Kitchens asked.

"He's out eatin'," the young man told him. "But I'm his deputy, Billy Bass. What can I do for you?"

"I'm from Rakestraw's outfit," Kitchens replied. "He sent me in to deliver a message to that federal man that's waitin' here for him."

The deputy just looked at him for a moment, nodding his head gravely. "Your herd's close by, huh?" he asked.

"No more'n half a day's drive out. Ned says he don't want no trouble, but he aims to deliver them personal, come hell or a hailstorm."

"There'll be trouble," the deputy told him. "It's thick in the wind like the smell of a sagegrass fire. This Parkman, he ain't a backin-down sort of man. He's killed four already that tried to stop him, an' he'll kill you, too, if you set your mind to take him."

"I jus' come to talk," Kitchens insisted, glancing down to draw attention to his empty holster. "Where can I find him?"

As the deputy came around the desk, he said, "Follow me. I'll show you." The two of them went outside, and Billy pointed toward the east, indicating the hill where Parkman was maintaining his second day of silent sentinel duty.

Kitchens glanced over at the deputy in confusion and asked, "What in tarnation's he doin' up there?"

"Nobody knows for sure," Billy said. "But he's been up there two days now, an' he's got the whole town antsy as hell. It's like waitin' for a tornado to hit or somethin'."

"Is he crazy like they say? Some of the hands we met said he'd sooner gun a man down than eat gravy. They talk like he eats horseshoes for breakfast an' spits out nails."

"He's not crazy," Billy Bass said solemnly. "I spent some time around him, an' he's square. But he's tough all right, an' right now he's pissed 'cause all he's done since he hit town is gun down bushwhackers an' fight to stay alive. You watch your step if you aim to go up there."

"Much obliged," Kitchens muttered as the deputy turned and went back into the office. The young cowboy stood there for a moment longer, staring at the distant threatening figure of the U.S. marshal. This was a real bucket of trouble if there ever was one. Finally, his gaze wandered across the street to the batwing doors of an open saloon, and it took him only a moment to decide that he deserved a snoot full of courage before tackling this one.

An hour later as Ty Kitchens ambled out of the saloon and across the street to his horse, his attitude had not improved much, but he had become a little more philosophical about such things as death and the rotten twists of fate that life sometimes socked a man with. Hell, he thought, if he did have to go out, maybe this was a better way than out back of some border cantina with a whore's shiv wedged up under his rib cage.

He loosened his horse's reins from the rail, swung up easily onto its back, and turned without hesitation toward the statuesque figure on the hillside to the east. The marshal obviously spotted him as he left the edge of the town, but he made no movement as Kitchens crossed the half mile of open country between them. Even as the young cowboy got quite near, he could see no movement from the stern lawman except an occasional calculating flicker of his eyes. When he got within about ten feet, he reigned up and left both of his hands in plain sight, resting casually on the horn of his saddle. He was turned enough to the side that Parkman could see the empty holster dangling loosely at his side, and his rifle boot was tied unusually far back on his saddle.

"Rakestraw sent me," Kitchens said at last, trying his best to appear calm and unafraid. He didn't know exactly what sort of man he had expected to find here, but this marshal appeared to be nothing like the quick-triggered gunslinger that the men on the trail had described him to be. He was a pretty ordinary-looking fellow and could even have been taken for nothing more than just another working cowhand, except for the tarnished badge that was pinned above the left pocket of his plaid shirt.

"I'm sure glad to see that empty leather," the marshal said quietly. "There's been too much dyin' already. No need for you to go, too."

"We shore think the same about that," Kitchens told him with relief. "I'm jus' bringin' a message, an' then I'll be haulin' it out of here as peaceable as hell."

"What's the message?" Parkman asked.

"The boss says he's bringin' the herd in, but he won't let you take him," Kitchens said. "There won't be no trouble 'less you start it, but if you do, you'll have all you can handle an' then some."

Parkman simply nodded his head.

Kitchens waited for a moment, then finally decided to try a bit of logic. "Marshal, there's fourteen of us, countin' Rake an' the cook," he insisted. "Why would you want to go up against an outfit that size? It's just like beggin' us to kill you, an' nobody wants to do that unless we have to."

It seemed to Kitchens that he could see the hard lines of determination in Parkman's face soften slightly. "My mind's set in this matter, son," the marshal said quietly. "Them's some tough odds, for a fact, but don't none of us know what'll happen."

"At fourteen to one, it ain't hard to predict," Kitchens said.

"Mebbe not," Parkman said. "But you go on back an' tell your boss I'll be waitin'. He could still save some lives—his, mine, yours, nobody knows—if he'd just give up. He'll get a fair trial."

"I'll tell him, but he won't. He ain't a man to give in so easy."

"I 'spect we're two of a kind then," the marshal said. "That's too bad for somebody."

Kitchens did not return to town, choosing to start straight back and intercept the herd instead. As he topped a distant rise far to the south of Cornersville, he stopped his horse a moment and glanced back. Parkman was still where he had been, a distant dark dot on the rolling green landscape of the Kansas plains.

CHAPTER TEN

He spotted their dust cloud far to the south before he actually caught sight of any of the steers in the herd. He guessed that they were somewhere past the Arkansas crossing, and apparently Rakestraw had decided not to stop his herd there for the usual day of watering and grazing before bringing it on in. Parkman knew Rakestraw must be in nearly as big a hurry as anybody else to get this business out of the way.

Finally, the lead animals of the herd plodded in sight south of town, and soon the crew began turning them slightly to the west, heading them toward the large holding pens on that end of town.

Parkman kept his spot for a while longer, watching all that was going on, counting men and preparing himself mentally for the dangerous task ahead. During his two-day vigil here on the hilltop, he had considered countless ways that he might approach the job of arresting Rakestraw, but now that the time had come, he had no idea how he was going to handle it. The plain fact of the matter was that there was no good way to go about it. Any way you turned it, it still looked like what everybody had been saying all along. It was a suicide mission, custom-made for a self-destructive fool.

But what the hell.

Gripping the reins of President Grant in his left hand, he nudged the animal's husky shoulders with his knees and said, "Let's get to it, ol' fella." The big horse, as restless after the long hours of inactivity of his master, broke into a frisky trot as they started down the hill toward town.

When he neared the first buildings on the east side of Cornersville, Parkman checked the loads in both his rifles, then kept the Winchester out of the boot, holding it like a pistol in his right hand, pointed skyward. He had no idea what sort of reception he might get from the people in town, but he wanted to be ready for anything that might come along. He was not about to let anybody stop him now, not after all he had gone through to this point.

As he started past the first buildings, riding along the side of the railroad tracks right through the center of town, people began appearing from everywhere to stand silently on sidewalks and in the edge of the street to watch him. They acted almost as if he was some awful apparition whose appearance had been long dreaded here.

Parkman let his eyes rove the crowd freely, and each time his eyes met those of another man, he sent out an unmistakable message. *Leave me be or die.* Nobody offered to interfere with his progress, either by word or deed. They were afraid of him now, awed by his strange behavior and by the fact that he was still determined to go after Rakestraw against all odds.

He saw no one in front of the marshal's office as he approached, but when he was almost to it, two figures stepped out the door and paused on the board sidewalk. Wyatt Bass wore his neat brown suit with the jacket buttoned and his twin Colts out of sight. Slightly behind him and to one side was Billy Bass, wearing his sidearm and holding a rifle in his hands. The two stared up at him as he neared, one with resentment and distrust, the other with apprehension and uncertainty.

Ridge was about to ride on by, but then Bass called out to him. "Parkman! I'll have a word with you."

Ridge stopped his horse and turned to face the city marshal. "Hadn't we gone beyond that?" he asked. "You know there's only one way you can stop me now, an' I don't think you'll try it. You're not sure anymore that you could do it."

"I could do it," Bass said, but still he did not reach up to open the button of his jacket. "But I don't see much need. They'll be diggin' your grave before nightfall without me ever havin' to raise a finger."

Ridge could see the younger Bass brother fidgeting behind Wyatt, looking from one to the other of them in agitation. Finally he seemed to make up his mind about something and took a determined step forward. "I reckon I'll be goin' along, Ridge, if you'll have me," he told Parkman.

Bass's head whipped around and he gazed at his brother in sudden angry surprise. "No, Billy! This ain't our concern. If he's fool enough to go on, he goes alone."

Billy ignored his brother's orders as he stepped up to Ridge and said, "How about it, Marshal? Can you use an extra gun?"

"I could use a dozen right now, but one like you'll do good enough."

As they started on down the street, Ridge still on his horse and the deputy afoot, Bass called out sharply, "Billy. Get your tail back here *right now!*" But Billy kept going, not even bothering to respond with a turn of his head. Bass glanced at the faces of the people around him, seeming to notice for the first time all the witnesses that there had been to this scene. But none of them were willing to look him in the eye now, as if each was sharing in a slight way the shame he felt. He spun at last and marched off down the street toward the Dixie Darling.

When Parkman and Billy reached the beginning of the cattle pens at the end of the long street, Parkman dismounted and tied the reins of his horse to a hitching rail nearby. He did not expect Rakestraw to make a break for it, not after he had come this far, but the marshal wanted to have his mount there just in case. To their left was a short row of wooden buildings most of which were used by the cattle companies as offices. On the right was a six-foot-deep ditch which was a part of the town's primitive sewer run-off system. Parkman noted both details carefully, glad to have cover available on both sides if it was needed. A few hundred yards away they could see the Circle Bar G crew herding the last of the cattle into one of the huge holding pens.

"What's the plan, Ridge?" Billy asked.

Parkman looked at his younger companion solemnly and said, "Mainly we jus' try to stay alive, I reckon." Then pointing with his rifle at the nearest building on the left, he said, "I want you up on the roof of that building with your rifle. We'll wait here for them, an' if trouble starts up, try to kill Rakestraw first. This is all his doin', an' if any man has to die, it should be him."

"Now wait a minute, Ridge . . ." Billy began to argue.

But Parkman interrupted him. "I hadn't got time to argue, Billy," he said. "Either you do it my way, or you back off an' stay out of the way. Make a quick pick which way you want it."

"I'm with you right down the line, Ridge," the young man said, turning toward the building without further protest.

Parkman was sure that Rakestraw and his crew must have spotted them by now, but the cowboys were still busy with the cattle, so he just stood in the middle of the street and waited, his rifle at the ready.

When the last double gates of the pen were swung shut, the cowboys began one by one to dismount, and then started strolling over in his direction. The marshal could tell by the way they acted that this was not the first fight they had been in together. Without any instructions they spread out in a wide ragged line and stopped about a hundred feet from where Parkman stood. In a moment one man came from the pens and walked to the center of the line of men. Ridge knew that must be Rakestraw.

"I figger you're Parkman," he said. His voice was firm and loud, but there was no hint of anger or animosity in it.

Rakestraw was about as Ridge had pictured him—a tall, angular man in his late forties, all lean, hard muscle and bone from a lifetime of strenuous, outdoor work. He wore a dirty plaid shirt and denim trousers with the heavy rawhide chaps which were a necessity on the trail strapped to the insides of his legs. A gunbelt hung around his waist with the holster turned forward on the left side to be clear of the chaps, and he carried a Henry rifle easily in his right hand. Beneath the wide brim of his sweat-stained Stetson, his leathery face held a look of almost friendly concern and regret. His squint-eyed gaze was intent and cautious.

"You got that right," Parkman told him. "An' if you're Ned Rakestraw, then you're under arrest for shooting Colonel William Shacklee in El Paso. I got a warrant here in my pocket if you'd like to take a look at it." As he spoke, his eyes scanned the wide line of men he faced, trying to decide which might be the jumpy ones who could be expected to go for their guns first.

"No need," Rakestraw said. "I killed him all right. I shot him dead as a hammer, but it was a fair fight. My men here can bear witness that he didn't give me no choice in the matter."

"I hope to hell that's the truth," Parkman said. "I never liked hangings. But I'm not the one that does the judgin' in these things. I jus' take 'em in . . . when I'm able."

"Did you get my message, Parkman?" the trail boss asked.

"Yup. But I was hopin' you'd changed your mind by now. If you come along willin', it'd save a lot of fuss, an' likely some lives, too. There's been too much trouble already."

"Sorry," Rakestraw said, and the tone of his voice showed that he actually was. For a moment they just stood there staring at one another, each wishing there was some possible way for them to avoid the inevitable next step. But things had gone too far. It was no longer possible for either of them to back away and find another way around this predicament. It only remained for the first gun to be drawn, the first shot to be fired—

but neither of them was willing to be the one that made that happen.

"Watch it, Ridge!" Billy Bass shouted out suddenly from his rooftop position. An instant after he yelled, his rifle began to bark. His shots were aimed at a man who had been lurking behind Rakestraw's crew back near the cattle pens. As the bullets connected, the man dropped the rifle he had been aiming, spun drunkenly, and collapsed to the ground.

Immediately the whole area was thrown into chaos. Parkman dived to the left, rolled once, and came to his feet running. A multitude of shots were flying in his direction. Rakestraw's crew scattered in several directions at once, but none of them tried to close the distance between them and the lawmen, not wanting to charge straight into the muzzle of Billy's deadly Winchester.

Ridge snapped off four of the six rounds in his Colt as he raced to the safety of the nearby buildings, and he thought he caught a glimpse of a couple of men going down before he crashed through the door of the buyer's office. Above him, Billy's rifle quieted, and an instant later the deputy came leaping through an open window at the back of the building.

"They were circling fast," Billy explained breathlessly. "Another minute an' they would have been in position to pick me off."

By then shots were ripping through the thin plank walls of the office from all directions. Keeping as low as possible, the two lawmen began moving the furniture inside against the walls to provide them some protection against the withering assault. They only stopped for a breath when Ridge had the heavy oak desk in position across the doorway, and Billy was safely behind a thickly padded sofa along the opposite wall.

"You all right?" Ridge asked, casting a glance over his shoulder at his companion.

"I ain't hit yet, if that's what you mean," Billy told him. "But I don't expect to stay that way for long. There's four sides to this place, an' only two of us to watch 'em."

"We'll jus' have to keep movin' around," Ridge told him. "I don't figger they'll be all that anxious to charge in here." He moved to one side window, peeked out cautiously, and snapped off a couple of rounds. His shots kicked up some dirt at the feet of a man who was racing to safety behind a horse trough.

"Sorry I had to be the one to kick things off," Billy said. "I kept watchin' that feller ease through the pens, an' I thought he was just comin' up to join the others. But when he lifted that rifle an' put his sights on you, I had to drop him."

"I can't hardly fault you for savin' my life," Ridge said easily. "An' anyway, it was about to start one way or another. Did you see how many went down?"

"Three, I think. I got one in the pens an' one other. You connected once on the run."

Parkman peered up cautiously and spotted one of the cowboys spread-eagled and unmoving a hundred feet away.

Then he eased back over to the desk and took a look out the front door. From there he could see another of Rakestraw's crew trying weakly to crawl to safety.

Ridge ducked back behind the desk and called out loudly, "Rakestraw?"

"Yeh?" came the distant answer from the direction of the drainage ditch.

"Pick up your wounded if you want 'em," Ridge said. "Ain't no use in them jus' layin' out there sufferin'."

"You won't shoot?"

"Not if you don't try nothin'."

Ridge peeked up again and saw two men come cautiously out from their cover. They ran to the wounded man, picked him up by both arms, and dragged him hurriedly out of the line of fire. As soon as they were in the clear, the Texans began hurling another barrage at the building, but both Ridge and Billy were well protected and were not hit.

When the firing had subsided once more, Ridge risked another look out. He saw a man dash from behind a stack of hay bales and start off in the direction of the ditch. Ridge snapped off two shots and the runner doubled over and tumbled out of sight into the ditch. On the other side, Billy raised up to fire a couple of times with his rifle, then ducked back down, fumbling in his shirt pocket for more cartridges.

"I didn't bring enough shells for a long fight," Billy said worriedly. "I didn't know it would turn into somethin' like this."

"Jus' make what you got count," Ridge told him. "I didn't figger on this myself, but we ain't got much choice now but to sit tight an' wait. It's their move."

CHAPTER ELEVEN

Over the next few minutes the gunfight fell into a pattern of the Texans sniping constantly to keep the lawmen captive in the cattle office and Ridge and Billy firing only rarely when they spotted a target.

Then, after a while longer, the shooting stopped completely. Ridge waited a moment behind the desk then finally raised up and took a look out the doorway. The street was still clear, and over by the drainage ditch he could see a couple of the cowboys peering up cautiously. But they were not looking in his direction.

Parkman moved carefully sideways until he could look back up the street toward town, and there he saw the reason for the pause in the fighting.

"Come here, Billy," Ridge said. "You've gotta see this."

Billy moved over and looked in the direction Parkman indicated. "It's Wyatt," he mumbled in surprise. "An' he's got his fightin' clothes on."

"But no guns," Parkman noted. "What in the hell's he up to?"

"I don't know," Billy said. "I can't recall ever seeing him outside without a sidearm on or a rifle in his hand."

Bass stood completely still in the middle of the

street. Instead of the brown suit he had on earlier, he was now wearing a faded flannel shirt and denim trousers. He looked unnatural in those clothes, and incomplete without his customary gunbelt strapped around his waist. Far behind him down the street, at what was a reasonably safe distance from the flying lead, it seemed that half the town had gathered to witness what was going on.

Then the city marshal began walking forward, his long legs closing the distance to the battleground in a confident, almost leisurely, fashion. When he was within about fifty feet of the drainage ditch, and about the same distance from the buildings where Ridge and Billy were, he stopped and called out, "Rake? Where you at?"

From his position down in the edge of the ditch, Rakestraw raised his head up and said, "I'm over here, Wyatt."

"I'm sorry to see this, Rake," Bass told his friend. "I wasn't goin' to meddle in this business between you an' Parkman, but it's gone too far now an' I mean to put a stop to it. Give it up, Rake. Turn yourself in before any more of your men are killed. I'll take you back to El Paso myself an' make sure they treat you square down there."

"Can't do it, Wyatt," Rakestraw told him firmly. "They've drawn blood already, an' now there has to be a reckonin'."

"My brother's in there," Bass said. It was not a plea exactly, but more a mere statement of fact.

"I thought that was Billy I spied up on that roof," the trail boss said. "Damn, I hate that, Wyatt. But he's done plugged two of us already. It was his rifle killed my cook over yonder in the pens, an' he laid ol' Blaine

Tomes out, too. He chose his fight, an' now he's stuck with it. You'd best just go back an' have a drink or two 'til this thing is settled."

Even from a distance Ridge could see the big lawman tense with anger at Rakestraw's defiance. "I'm gettin' damned tired," Bass exploded, "at everybody tellin' me lately what I will an' won't do right here in my own town. I jus' won't have it anymore. That's all there is to it!" He took another threatening step forward and pointed his finger at the Texas trail boss and his crew. "Now, Rake," he ordered, "you an' your men lay them guns of yours aside an' come on out here. Give it up."

Rakestraw calmly raised the Henry and fired a shot which plowed a six-inch furrow in the dirt between the city marshal's feet. The shot seemed to have no more effect on the tall lawman than if his opponent had thrown a pebble at him.

"Then it's a fight, Rake?" Bass asked.

"It's a fight."

Bass spun on his heels and strode off down the street. Within a moment he had reached the crowd of bystanders and began shoving his way roughly through them.

Bass's departure seemed to signal an end to the temporary truce, and a moment later the Texans began hurling a fresh volley of shots at the besieged lawmen.

By then the ammunition situation was becoming critical for Ridge and Billy, and at last Ridge told the young deputy not to fire anymore unless a charge began. There was no telling how long this thing might last, and they would need every round they had if the fighting became close-in. By what he had told Bass,

Rakestraw had indicated that he and his crew meant to have their revenge for the men Ridge and Billy had already downed.

As moments passed, the activity around the small building began to increase. The two besieged lawmen could not tell exactly what was going on, but on all sides, members of the Circle Bar G crew were racing from one bit of cover to another, apparently jockeying for better positions from which to make their final assault.

"They must be gettin' ready to rush us," Billy speculated grimly from the other side of the building.

"Yeh," Ridge agreed, "Either that or put the torch to this place. If I was them, that's what I'd do. Burn this shack down right slap dab on top of our heads."

"You sure know how to comfort a guy in a tight situation," Billy grumbled.

"Wal, you've got to think like your opponent," Ridge told him, "if you have any hopes of stopping him from doin' what he plans. But don't worry too much. From what was jus' said out there, I have an idea we haven't seen the last of your brother yet. Looks like he finally might come around an' start doin' the kind of job he shoulda been doin' all along."

"I hope so, Ridge," Billy said quietly. The shooting had lulled again, and the young deputy was sitting with his back to the heavy sofa, jamming extra rounds into the magazine of his rifle. As Ridge watched, Billy emptied the last of his bullets from his shirt pocket, loaded them in the gun, and looked up bleakly.

"Ever since you been here, Ridge," Billy admitted at last, "I've been confused. You know, since I was just twelve or thirteen, I've been reading great things about

my brother Wyatt, an' not just in the letters we got
from him out here. I was always finding dime novels
written about him, an' stories in magazines an' news-
papers telling what he did.

"Can you imagine the effect that sort of thing has on
a young teen-age boy? To be reading whole books
written about his brother's adventures? Hell, back then
if I'd been told he killed six men with one shot or run
the whole Mexican Army out of Texas by himself, I
would have never thought to doubt it. Then, when I
got old enough an' Wyatt sent word back that I could
come West an' learn to be a lawman under him, it
would've taken an act of Congress to keep me on the
other side of the Mississippi River.

"An' even after I came here, a lot of that same hero
worship stuck with me. He was an' still is one of the
best lawmen I've ever seen. The things he can do with
a gun are nothing short of incredible, an' there doesn't
seem to be one single ounce of fear or doubt in his
whole being. Even after all this time, it was still next to
impossible for me to believe he was capable of making a
mistake, that he might occasionally shoot a man un-
justly or make an error in judgment in a critical situation. I just didn't want to believe it was possible. Even
after you came."

"I never set out to destroy any of the admiration you
had for your brother," Ridge assured him quietly. "I
jus' came here to do a job, an' I couldn't let even him
stop me when I found out he stood on the other side."

"I know that, Ridge," Billy said. "I don't fault you
any for what you've done here. It was comin' anyway.
You just made it come faster, an' maybe that's a good
thing." He paused a moment and watched Ridge pile

tobacco on a paper and then roll it into a small, tight cigarette. "Smoke?" Parkman asked, offering the bag of tobacco.

"I wish I did right now," Billy said. Parkman nodded his head, understanding the feeling, glad of the instant of comfort the cigarette provided as he put it between his lips and drew in a mouthful of smoke.

"I think when I finally realized all the truth about Wyatt," Billy went on at last, "was a time that had nothing to do with you. It was that night that Wyatt beat up that cowboy, an' then I sat up all night downstairs in the Dixie Darling so that fellow's friends couldn't come in an' get to Wyatt. I did a lot of thinking that night, an' somewhere along the way a part of my hero worship for my older brother just withered up an' died. It's like I suddenly realized that he is just a man, that he can and will make mistakes along the way like anybody else.

"An' then all of a sudden I realized that I didn't have to work so hard tryin' to make myself just like him. I realized that to be my own man, the way I am, was all right, too. And that same night I realized that when the time came for you to go after Rakestraw, I had to go with you. It was the right thing to do, no matter what Wyatt might say."

Ridge didn't answer but nodded his head in understanding, drawing an odd comfort from the younger man's admissions. It had plagued him often in recent days that he had forced a barrier to arise between the two brothers, and this explanation relieved some of that worry. Perhaps, he decided, he had much less to do with it than he had imagined. As Billy said, the barrier would probably have arisen someday anyway, even if he had never set foot in Cornersville.

Parkman was distracted from his reflections by renewed activity at the edge of the ditch in front of him. A tall, husky man with shoulders like a bull's rose up at the edge of the ditch and drew back a flaming torch, apparently hoping to be able to throw it across the hundred feet of open space to the small office building. With some regret Ridge planted the sights of his rifle in the middle of the man's chest and squeezed off a round. The shot caught the cowboy in mid-throw, slamming his body backward into the ditch. The torch sailed a few feet in front of him, then landed harmlessly in the open area between them.

Back behind him, Billy fired his rifle once, then again, muttering a quiet curse under his breath.

Ridge did a little quick calculation to himself. They had already killed or wounded anywhere from four to six of Rakestraw's men, leaving only eight or ten to remain in the battle. From what he could tell, about half of them were lined up along the ditch facing him, with the rest scattered in various other places around the building. He wondered how many more men Rakestraw would be willing to sacrifice for the sake of honor and revenge. Judging from the quick impression Ridge had formed of the trail boss, he guessed that these losses must be eating at Rakestraw's conscience like a cancer.

But he was in too deep to stop now. Hell, they all were. By their own separate actions and judgments, all the participants had set this deadly drama in motion, but now fate had taken over. None of them any longer had any choice but to keep on fighting until they either died or persevered . . . and there would be no real winners. In the end there would only be those who lived and those who did not.

A flurry of rapid gunfire from the edge of town caught Ridge's attention, and it took him only a moment to realize that the shots were not being aimed at him and Billy. The sudden assault on their flank threw the men in the ditch into confusion. Soon they began running lengthways down it, working their way back toward the cattle pens and the horses they had left tied several hundred yards away.

Then Wyatt Bass came into view, and Ridge was struck immediately with the magnificent fearlessness which enabled him singlehandedly to drive five capable, armed men before him with his solitary charge. He worked his way forward with almost mechanical precision, laying down a barrage for himself with rifle and handgun as he raced from one bit of cover to another. Seldom had Parkman seen a weapon ever fired with such speed and accuracy by a stationary man, let alone by one who was firing bent over and running right into the face of a deadly hail of gunfire such as Bass was now doing.

"Judas Priest!" Ridge muttered under his breath in awe. "Maybe he *could* run the whole Mexican Army out of Texas if he took a mind to!"

Across the building, Billy snapped off a couple of shots and then turned to call urgently over his shoulder, "They're pullin' out, Ridge! They've started back toward the pens!"

"I see it," Ridge said, "but I can't hardly believe it."

And yet the Texans were not making their withdrawal in complete chaos. After the first shock of the sudden assault by Bass, they settled down into a pattern of retreat which was almost military in its precision. Two or three men would race to a bit of cover, then pause there and begin firing back while their

companions ran past them and found cover of their
own. Eventually the effectiveness of their tactic caused
Bass to slow up his attack and spend more time pro-
tecting himself from their accurate rifle fire.

At last Ridge could stand the confinement of the
building no longer. Leaping over the desk and out into
the street, he began running a frantic zigzag course toward a stack of hay bales near the pens that had sheltered one of the Texans only moments before. A couple
of bullets slapped the dirt near him, fired from somewhere ahead and to the left, but he didn't waste any
random shots until he had reached the safety of the
hay bales. To his left, he saw Billy race forward and
dive for cover behind a ten-foot-long watering trough.
To the right, Wyatt Bass was already out of sight, moving along the far side of the ditch as he pursued
Rakestraw and the three or four men who were still
with him.

As Ridge paused a moment behind the hay to regain
his breath, two problems still gnawed at him. In a way,
they had already gained a temporary victory by escap-
ing the confinement of the cattle office building, but
even though they were out and the Texans were fleeing, he still had not accomplished the single task he
had been sent here to do, and that was to arrest Ned
Rakestraw. The cowboys were obviously on their way
to their horses so they could flee the town. If they were
able to do that, then all this killing would have been
for nothing, and Ridge would still be faced with the
difficult task of starting southward, trailing Rakestraw
back toward his home state.

The other problem was ammunition. His Colt had a
full load of six rounds in it, but only three spares remained in his pistol belt. He wasn't sure, but he

thought there were only two or three more bullets left in the magazine of his Winchester.

To his left Ridge saw Billy leap up from behind the trough and start running for the next bit of cover ahead. On the right several shots cracked beyond the pens and a man screamed out in agony. Ridge decided it was as good a time as any to do a little legwork himself. There was nothing that would bring any solution to the problems he faced except to keep moving forward, taking advantage of the momentum Bass had started, and to do his damnedest to reach those horses and stop Rakestraw before he ran out of bullets to do it with.

Billy seemed to be working his way around the edge of the pens on the left, and Wyatt was doing the same on the right, so Ridge decided to plunge right up the middle. He ran forward, vaulted the rail fence ahead, and ran straight into the milling herd of cattle that was confined there. The animals, already jittery because of the nearby gunfire, were none too happy about this intruder in their midst, but Ridge worked his way through them as quickly as possible, dancing from side to side to avoid being crushed between the animals, and occasionally dropping to his hands and knees to crawl through where he could not walk.

Moving as he was, he did not see the man ahead until he was almost on top of him. Their eyes met at the same time, and both were startled, not expecting to run into anybody out in the middle of the herd like this. Ridge dropped to his knees just as the other man's gun exploded. Then, peeking beneath the bellies of the two steers that separated them, Parkman fired, catching the man in the lower part of his stomach.

Packed as they were like pickles in a jar, the cattle

reacted to the two resounding shots. Ridge felt the panic flow through the herd around him, and one steer near him shifted suddenly sideways, knocking him to the ground. He narrowly missed having his foot stomped by one animal, then his arm by another. He knew his life would not last more than another moment unless he could somehow get up off the ground and to his feet. His rifle was quickly lost in the shuffle, then his pistol was knocked from his hand by a kicking hoof.

Reaching up desperately, Parkman grabbed ahold of the tail of a startled steer above him and hauled mightily. He could feel the absolute terror growing in the minds of the cattle around him, their eyes growing huge and desperate, their customary moos turning into prolonged bleats of panic. And then they were on the move, somehow all magically turned in one direction, fleeing in mindless abandon from the unknown demons that terrorized them.

Ridge had just managed to stand erect when the animal in front of him spun to join the stampede. Desperately, the marshal leaped astride the steer's back, his fingers digging into the rough cowhide for a handhold. As it began to run, the steer bucked and kicked frantically, attempting to free itself of the unknown weight on its back, but Ridge wrapped his legs around its middle and hugged them together with all his might.

He had no idea what direction they were going. His only awareness was of a sea of brown backs around him, thick choking clouds of grit and dust, and the incessant, deafening roar of hundreds of suddenly pounding hooves. Repeatedly, the sides of the animals nearby crashed against the one he was riding, smashing his legs painfully against the steer's unyielding ribs, but he would not let go.

In a minute, as the stampeding cattle continued to run in one direction uninterrupted, Parkman realized that they must have demolished the sides of the holding pens. And when they did not immediately encounter any buildings or the deep ditch, he knew that the stampede must be headed either west or south. They thundered away mindlessly, spreading out across the open prairie like a thick, dark cloud.

He felt the steer beneath him shift its weight sideways and saw its head snap around in another attempt to throw the unwanted weight from its back. The movement caught Ridge off guard and his handhold on the animal's side slipped. He reached out for one long, ivory horn, desperate to stay atop its back and avoid falling beneath the pounding hooves of the animals behind.

But the maneuver and the sudden shift in Parkman's weight threw the steer off balance and it began to fall. There was no time for any thought or action. As the steer went down, Ridge felt himself flying through the air, headed toward what he felt must be certain death. He hit the ground with a rib-snapping thud and his mind spun away sickeningly into a black void that he thought for certain must be the prelude to death.

CHAPTER TWELVE

The bleating penetrated through to his consciousness first. It was an insistent noise that bore into his delirium, demanding that he return from nothingness and realize that he was still alive. He knuckled his eyes like an infant before opening them, trying to clear the scum of dirt and dust away so that he could focus again. Then he stirred slightly, only enough to let him know that his body felt like a pounded steak. Slowly, the aches began to come into clearer focus, too . . . head, back, leg, hand . . .

Cautiously, he rose up onto one elbow and looked around. A dozen or so yards to the left an injured steer struggled pitifully to stand up on two front legs, its back legs twisted and bloody. That, he guessed, was probably the animal that had saved his life during the desperate ride through the stampede, and the same one which nearly took it from him with its clumsy bucking and pitching. Far to his left, the pounding of the stampeding cattle was fading. They might run for hours before stopping, or turn in the next minute and settle down to grazing. It was hard to tell about cattle that way.

He rose stiffly to his feet, more than a little surprised that both his legs still worked and that no bones seemed to be broken. Certainly, he should have been dead by now. It seemed like an hour ago that he had been wading through the cattle pens, but he realized that probably only a few minutes had passed. And then suddenly everything else began to come back to him, crashing into his jarred consciousness like a dumped ore wagon.

He had left a fight behind, a bloody struggle that was probably still going on. Immediately he was desperate to get back.

Judging from the wide swath of pulverized prairie grass around him, the herd had apparently plunged straight west out of town, then for some unknown reason turned to the northwest. Ridge had been carried more than a quarter mile from town and across a small rise before being thrown clear.

Ignoring the throbbing pain in his skull, left arm, and left leg, he started back at a clumsy trot. As he topped the rise, he saw the serpentine form of the drainage ditch a couple of hundred yards ahead of him. Beyond it, the scattered remnants of Rakestraw's crew were crouched down behind the carcasses of a few dead steers and the tangled remnants of their chuck wagon, still hurling lead in the direction of the deep ditch. Their horses were nowhere in sight. Probably they had panicked at the sight of the onrushing herd and had turned to race away with it.

But that only put the Texans in a more difficult situation. They had no way to flee now. Their only recourse was to stand and fight. Bullets began peppering around him as he approached the ditch, but he quickened his pace over the last hundred yards and ran in a random, zigzag pattern, partly out of evasiveness and partly because of the shooting pains that

raced up from his left ankle and burned their way
the entire length of his left leg. Maybe, he thought, he
had been a little hasty in his judgment that nothing
was broken down there.

When he reached the ditch, he dropped over the
rim and tumbled to the bottom clumsily. A few yards
away Billy Bass spun and aimed his revolver, but then
recognized Parkman in time to hold the shot.

"Ridge!" the young deputy exclaimed. "Where'd
you come from? I thought you'd lost it in the stampede."

"Not quite," Parkman told him, "but I jus' had
me one hell of a bareback ride."

Beside Billy lay his brother, propped up against the
ditchbank facing the scattered Texans nearby. Wyatt's
right arm lay slightly twisted by his side, bloodied
from the elbow down and idle like an irreparable piece
of equipment cast hastily aside. Far down his back on
the right side another bullet hole had bloodied the
back of his shirt and the tops of his trousers. The bank
of the ravine around him resembled a slaughterhouse
floor. But he still held one of the pearl-handled Colts
in his left hand and pointed cautiously toward the
distant opponents.

When he turned to face Parkman, Bass's face was
a mask of ill-concealed pain, but his sunken eyes still
communicated that familiar burning hatred. "You son
of a bitch," he muttered in a harsh, labored gasp.
"Can't nothin' kill you?"

"I might ask the same thing, Bass," Ridge responded
coolly. "Damn, man, shouldn't you be dead with that
many holes in you?"

"I ain't about to die 'til this thing's settled," Bass

responded testily. "Hell, if I went now, it'd give too many bastards too much satisfaction." His look told Ridge that he was clearly included in that group.

"Wal, how'd you get way the hell over here?" Ridge asked Billy. "The last I saw of you, you were on the other side of the pens."

"I'm not too clear on that myself," the deputy admitted. "When the herd broke down the fences, they started right at me, so I cut to the side an' run around behind them. Rakestraw's men had scattered in all directions by then, an' the only cover I could see was this ditch. When I got in it, I worked my way toward this end and found Wyatt here like this. I been tryin' to convince him to let me carry him back to town, but he won't go."

"Hell, they wouldn't let us get twenty feet before they'd be on us like hornets," Bass scoffed. "Where they are now, out in the open like that, we got 'em nailed down. They can't charge an' they can't run. They can't do shit."

Glancing over the rim of the ditch, Ridge saw that Bass's estimation of the situation was accurate. The overwhelming charge of the stampeding cattle had nearly cleared away every obstruction in the area, leaving the Texans with scant cover to maneuver behind. To their backs and to their left was only clear open prairie, and the nearest buildings of the town were over a hundred yards to their right.

A bullet furrowed the rim of the ditch as he ducked his head back down, but the Texans had just about quit shooting. Ridge guessed that by now they were probably running short of ammunition, too.

Then a distant shout sounded out across the open area. "Parkman?" Ridge recognized Rakestraw's voice.

"Yeh?" Ridge responded. "What do you want, Rakestraw?"

"Let's finish this, Parkman. You an' me."

Ridge glanced at the two men beside him, surprised and suspicious of the offer. In Bass's face he read the unmistakable glint of challenge.

"It's cost too much already, Parkman," Rakestraw continued. "I got five or six dead an' three wounded. That's enough. Let's have it out now an' be done with it."

Neither of the men with Ridge had yet commented, but in a moment Bass turned the pistol he held so the grip was extended toward Parkman.

"I noticed your empty holster," the city marshal said at last. "He's right. This is the way to end it."

Ridge accepted the pistol without hesitation, hefting it momentarily and admiring its action and balance. The grip was still sticky with fresh blood from Bass's wound, and he wiped it hastily on his shirt front. Then he picked up a handful of dust, ground it in his palm, and wiped it on the handle of the pistol to absorb the excess moisture. Finally, holstering the revolver, he stood up and scrambled up out of the ditch.

It was a risk. He realized that it would only take one scoundrel in Rakestraw's crew to pick him off before he had a chance to face the trail boss man to man. But, then, the whole thing had been a risk from beginning to end. He and the two men behind him were damned lucky to have survived this long, and if the battle went on, surely at least one of them would die. Bass wouldn't survive another twenty minutes if he didn't get those holes plugged up somehow.

From behind the hulking form of a dead steer fifty yards away, Ned Rakestraw rose to his feet. He slowly,

almost gently, laid his Henry across the side of the
animal, shifted his holster slightly around to the side,
and began to walk forward.

Ridge started forward, too, moving about twenty-
five feet from the edge of the ditch before stopping
again. Rakestraw closed the distance between them to
about fifty feet, then stopped and planted his feet wide
apart, braced and steady.

As he and Rakestraw stared intently into one
another's eyes, Ridge could not rid himself of the
feeling that this whole thing was a travesty. None of
this should be happening. None of these men should
have died, and he and Rakestraw should not now be
facing each other like this, each waiting to kill or be
killed.

The face of that man over there, though hard from
the things he had dealt with in life and the rugged
way he lived, was not the face of a killer. There was
a certain intelligence and integrity in his eyes, as well
as that same regret that Ridge had seen there when
they first talked to one another before the shooting
began. It was the face of a good man, but fate had
caught ahold of him, suddenly twisting his destiny and
turning his future to ashes. Ridge felt a deep regret
at having become a pawn of that fate, a piece of Rakestraw's ruin. His job seemed repulsive sometimes, but
even when that happened, he went ahead and did his
best anyway. That's what a man was supposed to do.

"I hate this," Ridge told the trail boss quietly.

Rakestraw nodded his head sadly, fully agreeing,
understanding the necessity and the tragedy of it. "It's
a damn shame," he said.

For a moment Ridge allowed his feelings to carry
him, but finally he began to pull his mind back under

control. No matter what else it might be, this was a situation where death was in the cards for one of the two men there, and he had to do his best to make sure that all the dying was done by somebody else. His eyes dropped away from Rakestraw's face, darting down to where his twitching fingers hovered within inches of his holstered revolver. Now, during these final moments of the fight, Rakestraw's steely nerves at last seemed to be failing him. Countless times before he had faced death, but this was probably the first time he had ever looked it squarely in the face and realized that it was truly about to claim him.

When the hand of the trail boss slapped suddenly at the grip of his revolver, Parkman turned everything over to a set of instincts honed keen by years of practice. All in an instant, the Colt slid easily and surely from the holster, the hammer was thumbed back as the barrel was raised, the trigger was squeezed, and the lethal chunk of lead raced away on its deadly mission.

It was never really a contest. Ridge knew it all the time, and so probably did Rakestraw. One man was a cowboy and the other a skilled technician at the craft of killing, however regretful he might feel about that side of his profession. But if both of them knew what the outcome of the shoot-out would be, they also realized that it was the Texan's time. He had to die.

The trail boss stood for a moment, staring ahead blankly, already dead from the .45 caliber bullet that had embedded itself in the center of his chest. Then slowly as his knees began to buckle and he started down, the pistol he held slipped from his fingers. He toppled forward like a felled oak, landing face down in the dirt.

Ridge stayed where he was and kept the Colt drawn as the remaining members of the Circle Bar G crew rose one by one from the places where they had been, but they ignored him as they moved silently forward toward the body of their fallen leader. They gathered around him a moment, talking silently among themselves, then slowly two of the men picked him up and started away.

Finally, one of the cowboys turned to Ridge and said, "Far as we're concerned, it's finished, Marshal. You feel the same?"

Parkman nodded his head.

"Then we'll be buryin' our dead now."

The marshal nodded again, then turned away. Behind him, Billy Bass was just beginning to help Wyatt up out of the ditch.

CHAPTER THIRTEEN

Though there were many other things about Cornersville that Ridge would be glad to leave behind him,
he knew that when he was gone he would certainly
miss the good meals he had enjoyed at Mabel Cain's
Café. After spoiling himself for more than two weeks
on her thick steaks, generous portions of fresh vegetables, and smooth, rich coffee, it would be a chore returning to the beans, bacon, and hardtack of the trail.

Those and other similar thoughts were running
through Ridge's mind as he sat near the back of
Mabel's Café, watching her quickly clear a recently
vacated table nearby. A man could do a lot worse for
himself than to settle down in one place with a woman
like her at his side, he thought. She was a strong, re-
silient woman, a hard worker, and the kind of person
who knew how to be tough as granite when that was
what the world demanded of her. She was a lady who
knew how to survive and get along no matter where
she was or what was thrown in her direction, and yet
she had also given Ridge a brief glimpse of another
side of her personality which he admired as well.
There was much tenderness and generosity laying dor-
mant within her spirit, waiting for just the right per-

son to come along who was worthy of receiving it. And besides all that, she could cook, too. Man, could she ever.

Mabel carried her tray of dishes into the back, then returned and took her customary seat across the table from him. "So you're dead set on leaving, then?" she asked. "Couldn't nothing convince you to stay on another day or so?" The trace of yearning and disappointment was clear in her eyes and her voice, but Ridge tried to act as if he did not notice.

"I reckon not, Mabel," Ridge told her softly. "My job's done here, an' Denver's wired they're holdin' another assignment for me there 'til I get back."

"They could keep on holding it awhile longer, Ridge."

"It's my job, Mabel. It's the way I live, an' I can't rightly say I'd want things any other way."

She nodded her head, near tears now, but understanding, too. That was another thing he liked about her. She understood things, about how a man was and all.

But the lapse into emotion was only a temporary one for Mabel. In an instant the smile returned to her face and the zest to her voice. "Well, I'll guarantee you one thing, Marshal Ridge Parkman," she told him. "You're somebody that I won't be forgetting for a spell. No sireee. By God, you're a real man in a time when it's getting harder and harder to find any such critter around anyplace."

"You're one helluva unforgettable lady, too, Mabel," Ridge assured her. "An' that kind don't exactly grow on trees, neither. I couldn't of done what I did here without your help."

"Okay. Okay. Enough of this backslapping. I see

your horse is a'stomping and a'champing to get on the way, so let's get these good-byes over."

"It's gettin' time," Ridge agreed.

"Take care, Marshal, and if you're ever back this way . . ."

"I'll stop in for sure. Good-bye."

President Grant was tied to the rail outside the café, saddled, packed, and ready to go. But Ridge still had one more stop to make before he could leave town. Taking the reins of the horse, he started walking down the street toward the Dixie Darling Saloon.

Matt Rikard gave him a sour look, but didn't question his reasons when he entered the saloon and announced that he wanted to see Wyatt Bass. The bartender went away for a moment, then returned and said, "Follow me."

Wyatt Bass seemed to have lost twenty pounds and gained ten years since Parkman had last seen him the day before following the shoot-out. Alone in his room, the famous lawman seemed practically swallowed up by the large feather bed on which he lay. Despite the heat, a light comforter was pulled up above his waist, and most of his chest was covered by a mass of white gauze bandages. Both his arms were out from under the comforter, laying idly at his sides, and his right arm was bandaged heavily from elbow to wrist. He seemed half asleep when Parkman entered, unmoving, his face expressionless, his gaze sunken and deathly. As he stared at Ridge, the hatred seemed to be gone from his eyes, but no other expression had moved in to replace it.

"Bad?" Ridge asked, pointing to the bandaged arm. Both knew what the loss of a right arm or hand meant to a man who made his living with a gun.

"Bad enough," Bass answered in a dull monotone. "The doc says the bones will mend okay and that the muscles will heal, but . . ."

There was no need for him to finish the statement. Ridge understood. Even if the arm healed completely and Bass regained full use of it, he would finish his life considering himself as a man with a bum arm. The slightest recurring stiffness, the most minute misshape of bone or defect of muscle, would be enough to slow his draw that vital fraction of a second. He could never go up against another man again with full confidence that he could outdraw him and kill him.

"It's a tough break," Ridge said, letting his gaze wander the room idly. Something about this meeting was nerve-jangling, but he had felt compelled to come here one final time before leaving Cornersville. He couldn't have explained quite why.

On the dresser lay the pearl-handled Colt .45, which Ridge had used to kill Ned Rakestraw. It was still where he had laid it yesterday when they carried Bass in here and sent for the doctor, still smeared with dirt and the darkening stains of Bass's blood.

"I don't want your pity, Parkman," Bass told him suddenly. "I don't want your apologies or your lectures or your good-byes or whatever the hell else you come here for."

"I didn't come here for none of those reasons," Parkman told him, though he realized he was lying somewhat about the pity part as he studied Bass, lying there on the bed, burning with his solitary hatreds and disappointments. Whatever else he might feel about the man, it was impossible not to feel a degree of pity for his present state. It was somehow like getting a shadowy vision into the future of a great figure after the years had robbed him of his stature and might.

"It must be to gloat, then," Bass sneered. "I'd rather have that than anything else. I can tolerate that. Hell, maybe I even owe it to you. I don't know anymore."

"I don't know why I came," Ridge admitted. "It jus' seemed like I had to for some reason. Hell, maybe I was hopin' you'd be up an' around already, all full of vinegar an' cocksure confidence like you was that first night I rode into town. The world needs men like that to look up to an' admire. Maybe I feel kinda rotten now 'cause not even meanin' too, I took that away from a lot of people. It jus' seems like there's a hole now where the image of Wyatt Bass used to be."

"You made a lot of different holes around this place," Bass said, not even seeming to recognize the veiled condescension in Parkman's statement. "But there'll be other heroes to come in an' take the place of the ones like me that can't cut it anymore. Billy accepted the town board's offer to become interim city marshal. Hell, maybe someday he'll be totin' around a bigger reputation than I ever thought about havin'."

"Maybe," Ridge said. "But I doubt it. He'll do a good job, all right. A damn good job. But I see him easin' through life kinda quiet like, not hardly ever drawin' no notice, but always there when folks need him to be. He hadn't got the style to be a legend." Ridge paused and stared at Bass a moment, then added, "I'd call that a lucky break for him."

Bass turned his head away, staring out the window at the hill where only two days before Parkman had kept his silent vigil above the town. Much had changed since that time. His life had suddenly and unalterably turned away from the course which he had been so confident that it was headed and without warning began plunging to depths that he never before imagined possible for himself. He wondered stoically how far down he would drop before he hit bottom and began the arduous task of pulling himself back up again.

Without Bass hardly even noticing, Parkman turned away and started for the door. But before he got out, the famous lawman stopped him one final time.

"Parkman?" When Ridge stopped and turned, Bass told him quietly, "I saw your draw out there when you shot Rakestraw. It wasn't near good enough. I could have killed you if we ever squared off."

"I never doubted it," Parkman replied. A fleeting grin played across his face, and then he was gone.

When the Wind Blows

A chilling novel of occult terror!

John Saul

author of *Suffer the Children*
and *Punish the Sinners*

To the Indians, the ancient mine was a sacred place. To the local residents, it was their source of livelihood.

But the mine contains a deadly secret—and the souls of the town's lost children. Their cries can be heard at night, when the wind blows—and the terror begins.

A DELL BOOK $3.50   (19857-7)

DELL'S ACTION-PACKED WESTERNS

Selected Titles

SOLO

by **JACK HIGGINS**

author of The Eagle Has Landed

The pursuit of a brilliant concert pianist/master assassin brings this racing thriller to a shattering climax in compelling Higgins' fashion.

A Dell Book $2.95   (18165-8)

Dell Bestsellers